WHEN THE WAR CAME TO HANNAH

ALSO BY JANE S. CREASON

Fiction

The Heron Stayed

WHEN THE WAR CAME TO HANNAH

Jane S. Creason

Printed in the United States of America.

ISBN: 978-1-4269-6183-0 (sc)
ISBN: 978-1-4269-6184-7 (e)

Trafford rev.03/30/2011

 www.trafford.com

North America & International
toll-free: 1 888 232 4444 (USA & Canada)
phone: 250 383 6864 ♦ fax: 812 355 4082

Dedicated to the Swengels and the Nakanes

who lived their own version of this story

Chapter 1

The rattling yellow bus bounced down the gravel road as Old Henry jerked the steering wheel right and left, vainly trying to miss the biggest puddles. The tops of the little kids' heads appeared and disappeared above the high-backed seats in the front. Their squeals blended with yells from the older boys in the back. Holding my lips tight, I struggled to keep the oatmeal, which Mama insisted I eat, in my queasy stomach.

The bus lurched to a stop in front of a small house with peeling white paint. Old Henry blew the horn, two short blasts followed by one long one. When no one appeared immediately, he honked again, pulled out a pocket watch on a braided leather strap, and held it up high.

"One, two, three," the little kids shouted in unison as the second hand moved.

At the count of fifteen, Johnny Crow walked out the door and down the sagging front steps. The little kids cheered, as they did every morning, and kept counting. Johnny sauntered across the muddy yard with that smile on his face that he thought was irresistible and I thought was obnoxious. At twenty-eight, with two seconds to spare, he stepped onto the bus.

"Morning," he said, grinning at us and ignoring Old Henry, who stared straight ahead.

As Johnny started down the aisle, he ran his fingers through his straw-colored hair, tipped up his square chin, and raised his arm like a boxer who'd won a match. The cheers got louder. Glaring at us in the wide rearview mirror above his head, Old Henry slid the watch back into his pocket and rammed the gearshift into first. The bus jumped forward.

Sitting alone, I stared out the dirty window, watching mile after mile of familiar fences and fields slip by. I knew every face of the flat Midwestern land as the weather and the seasons painted it. I'd watched the green of late summer change to the gold and bronze of fall and then to the shimmering white of freshly fallen snow. The ugly, dingy gray of a winter thaw that morning seemed to fit the unlucky date on the calendar. It was Friday, the thirteenth of February, 1942.

Suddenly, the bus dropped over the little incline near Red Fox Creek, squarely hitting three slush-filled holes at the bottom. Shrieks came from the front as small bodies bounced around like rag dolls. Several metal lunch pails crashed to the floor. Frantically, I grabbed for my satchel and missed. It landed on the muddy floor with a thud. Ignoring the chaos behind him, Old Henry turned on the wipers to clear the blobs of gray-brown slush from his windshield. I looked at my beautiful blue satchel all smeared with mud from the many feet that had walked across soggy yards and down rutted lanes.

"Lord, I hate this bus ride," I said to no one in particular as I unbuttoned my coat to get the freshly ironed hankie in my dress pocket.

Using the hankie to clean my satchel would mean trouble at home. Mama set great store in my being a dignified young lady, and somehow clean handkerchiefs and straight posture and correct grammar and a hundred more things that were very important to her had to be remembered by me. When she saw the dirt, she'd frown and say, "My stars, Joanna, what on earth did you do this time?"

Looking at the hankie, I hesitated. Then, despite the possible consequences, I wiped the mud off my satchel, folded the dirt to the inside, and stuffed the hankie back into my dress pocket.

Unbuckling the straps on the satchel, I peeked inside to check the valentines in their white envelopes. There were twenty-one small store-bought cards and four big ones I'd painstakingly made myself from shiny red paper and lacy white hearts. Two of those were for Gloria Van Holt and Betty Jean Jones, and the verses I'd composed for them were identical since they were both my best friends. The third valentine was for my eighth grade teacher, Miss Franklin. Reaching inside, I carefully pulled out the fourth big envelope and held it close. It was blank on the outside, but inside the fancy card I'd written,

Roses are red, violets are blue.

You do not know, but I love you true.

I hadn't signed it. I knew what I was going to do with that valentine.

My heart began to race, and my face was getting hot. Quickly, I slipped the envelope back into the satchel. Hoping to hide my cheeks, I hunched my shoulders and turned up my coat collar. Blushing was the curse of my life. I blushed when I was mad or sad, embarrassed or excited, alone or in a group, and I blushed whenever I thought about Bill Elliott.

The bus careened around a corner and headed east toward town on the smoother concrete county road. I stared out the window, hoping my face would cool and wondering if my feet on the unheated floor would freeze with all the blood rushing to my face. It was three more miles to town with only the Isaacson twins to pick up. As usual, they were standing beside the road since Old Henry had left them twice when they'd missed his thirty-second deadline. With everyone aboard, we moved past the Steinbrawns' cattle herd, which was huddled together against the biting wind, and wound through a woods with shrinking, dirty snowdrifts beneath the leafless trees.

Then, without warning, Old Henry hit the brakes once, twice, a third time harder. I grabbed the seatback in front of me with one hand, tightened the grip on my satchel with the other, and begged my breakfast to stay in place. Two more lunch pails hit the floor. The little kids chattered excitedly and pressed their faces against the windows.

"How come you turned?" Johnny said to Old Henry as the bus headed north on Mill Pond Road. "No kids live up here."

Old Henry drove on.

"How come you turned?" Johnny said more loudly.

Johnny Crow, who seemed to believe that he was the leader of our eighth grade class and the entire school, wasn't used to being ignored. With all eyes on him, he rose and squared his broad shoulders.

"Why did you turn!" he demanded.

Old Henry said nothing.

I was beginning to enjoy the drama. However, before it could continue, Taylor Bensen, another boy in our class, broke the tension.

"I think I see someone standing by the mailbox at the old Herrin place, a girl, maybe," he said.

I strained to make out the figure through the grime on the window. When the bus stopped, all of us were quiet, our attention riveted on the door as it squeaked open.

"Is this the bus to Ten Oaks Elementary in Hannah?" a voice from outside said.

"Sit," Old Henry said.

I stared—everyone stared—as a tall, slender girl with the reddest curliest hair I'd ever seen climbed aboard.

She looked at us, then grinned. "I'm Gretchen Bocher," she said as she walked down the aisle and took the seat across from me.

Since staring and raising eyebrows were silent activities, the rest of the ride was uncharacteristically quiet. Minutes later, Old Henry brought the bus to an abrupt stop in front of the two-story white frame schoolhouse and swung the door open.

"Out," he said.

The little kids bounced down the steps and lined up on either side of the walk like spectators along a parade route. A new kid, especially a tall red-haired girl, was worth staring at some more.

Next came Gretchen. Pausing by Old Henry, she said, "Thank you for the ride, sir."

Then looking calm and confident, as if unaware that dozens of eyes were on her, she climbed off the bus and strode toward the school's red double doors. I was impressed since I would've been as shaky as jelly.

"Wonder which parent is the carrot?" Johnny said loudly from behind.

Snickers came from here and there as we trudged up the creaky wooden staircase. Once more my face was turning scarlet, but the blushing was for her. She, however, appeared to hear nothing. There was no embarrassed flush on her pale cheeks. She rounded the landing and climbed the last half-flight, stopping at the top only long enough to check the signs above the two doors. Fifth and sixth on the right, seventh and eighth on the left. She entered left.

A few students from town were already in the room, hovering around the big valentine box we'd decorated with red paint and lace during the week. They stopped to stare. Ignoring them, Gretchen walked directly to Miss Franklin, her right hand outstretched.

"I'm Gretchen Bocher. I'm new, from Chicago most recently, California before that. I'm in the eighth grade. Where should I sit?" she said in a rush.

Miss Franklin's look of surprise changed into a broad smile as they shook hands. "Well, Gretchen, welcome to our school. There's an empty desk over there."

The rest of us began to move around, though still keeping a close eye on Gretchen as she arranged the books for eighth grade in her desk. In the cloakroom, we hung up our coats and sweaters on the assigned hooks, lined up our galoshes below them, and shoved our lunch boxes, mittens, and scarves into wooden cubby holes on the opposite wall. The smell of damp wool filled the small room.

Standing in the middle of the cloakroom, Johnny was solemnly shaking hands all around. "I'm Jonathan Alvin Crow, most recently from Hudson Crossing. I'm in the eighth grade," he said in a tone mocking Gretchen's.

Then Seth and Warren Isaacson, seventh graders, came in, and there was more handshaking going on than at a political rally.

Three other boys lined up and addressed an invisible Old Henry. "Thank you for the ride, sir," each one said in turn.

I ducked out of the cloakroom right before Miss Franklin and Gretchen entered it. My face was still burning. I was halfway to my desk when I remembered the muddy handkerchief in my pocket. Maybe I could rinse out the mud.

I dashed through the door, down the steps, and out into the sharp wind. The pump was a few steps away from the sidewalk. There was a bit of water in the bucket beneath the spout. Shivering, I plunged my hands through the thin coat of ice on top and gave the hankie a good scrubbing. The dirty spots lightened considerably.

As I turned to go back into the schoolhouse, I saw Gloria and Betty Jean running across the schoolyard.

"Wait up, Joanna," Gloria yelled.

Betty Jean stopped and stared. "Are you crazy? Where's your coat?"

"I came outside to rinse out my hankie. It got muddy when I cleaned off my satchel. Old Henry was so wild this morning everything hit the floor. And you know what Mama says about me getting dirty."

"Let me see it," Betty Jean said.

"Maybe she won't notice," Gloria said as they examined the faint spots.

I shrugged. "I'm almost sorry I ever turned fourteen," I said. I was certain Mama's determination that I act properly had increased since my birthday in January.

"But at least you've got the satchel," Gloria said.

It was a gift from Grandma Grey, who seemed to know how to choose something special. It was the envy of the eighth grade girls, about the only thing I'd ever owned that anyone else wanted.

Overall, I was not the sort that inspired envy. So-so singing voice. So-so ball player, not picked first, not picked last. So-so artist, not outstanding like Betty Jean or awful like Johnny, who still drew trees resembling lollipops. A good student with a good vocabulary and good manners, which were Mama's doing. She'd gone to college a year, her one shining achievement, and if she could polish me up, I might become her second. But no one envied me for that.

I gave the hankie a final snap to shake out the last drops of water, then slid it into my pocket.

As we hurried toward the door, I said, "I have something to tell you. There's a new girl in eighth grade, from California. She rode the bus in. She has the reddest–"

The old iron bell on top of the school began to clang.

"I'll tell you more later," I shouted over the noise.

After we entered the classroom, Gloria and Betty Jean took a long look at Gretchen before heading for the cloakroom, where Johnny was still shaking hands. I heard "carrot" over and over as more town kids came in. I went directly to my desk.

"You aren't amused," a voice nearby said.

I looked up. Taylor was sitting at his desk in front of mine. He wasn't smiling.

I'd known Taylor forever since the Bensens lived a mile from us. I didn't think of him as a best friend like Gloria or Betty Jean since he was a boy, but he'd always had an uncanny way of knowing how I felt. Sometimes it could be annoying.

"Just because I'm not over there, trying to win an acting award like some clowns in this class, doesn't mean I'm not amused," I said, irritated.

"Touchy, Joanna."

"If this is all so much fun, how come you got out of the cloakroom in record time today, too?"

Turning my back on Taylor, I scooped up all my valentines, except the special one, which I slipped into my other pocket, and walked to the red box. As I dropped the envelopes through the top slot, I noticed Gretchen looking at the books on the corner shelves. They were Miss Franklin's own books, which she lent to any of us who wanted to read them. Few asked.

Then, with my heart thudding in my ears and my hands shaking, I walked back toward my desk. Pretending to sneeze, I stopped by Bill Elliott's desk, pulled my hankie from my pocket—I hadn't planned on it being wet—and dropped it. When I bent over to retrieve it, I quickly slipped the anonymous valentine inside the open front of his desk. As I stood up, I swiped my nose with the hankie, stuffed it back into my pocket, and nonchalantly looked around. The cloakroom was still crowded with handshakers. I didn't think anyone had seen me, and I prayed no one could hear my heart, especially Taylor. There were some things he didn't need to know.

The final bell was clanging when Bill rushed in. My heart pounded louder, and I wondered what shade of red my cheeks were. Bill took off his gray coat and quickly joined the other latecomers who were dropping their valentines into the box. I stared. He was tall with dark curls, deep blue eyes, and pale skin. I watched him walk to his seat, two rows over and one seat up from mine.

I'd adored Bill since the first day he'd walked into our seventh grade class over a year before. First, he'd been sweet on Gloria, and my heart had ached as he carried her books to and from school. Rosie Marconi was next, then Doris Armstrong, Hazel Evans, Clara Janke, Patty O'Brien, Alice Kramer, and Agnes Fischer. Sometimes I despaired, certain I was the only girl Bill hadn't noticed.

Actually, there were several of us left. Betty Jean wasn't interested. She'd never cared about anyone except Karl Hoffmann. And Ida Jo Powers, no boy ever liked her. She was twice as big as any of us. She spit on her hands before she knocked the ball through the trees about every time she batted, and she could swear. There was Kathleen, number eight of the eleven Fitzhenry kids. Every day she came to school in the same yellow-flowered dress, clean and ironed on Monday, wrinkled and smelly by Friday. I anguished over why I was in such company.

I knew I didn't have shiny blonde hair like Gloria or natural curls like Clara or a tiny cute nose like Patty. But my thick brown hair was neatly braided, and Papa always said my dark eyelashes made my blue eyes shine. Surely, Bill had noticed me. True, the valentine in his desk was anonymous, but I hadn't tried to disguise my penmanship. He had to know how long I'd been waiting.

At eight o'clock, Miss Franklin stood up from her desk chair, and so did the class. There was immediate, reverent silence. We faced the flag with hands over our hearts and pledged in unison. Though the ceremony had been repeated by us every morning since we'd entered first grade, even the rowdiest of the boys stood with a straight back as we solemnly recited the pledge. Only two months before, the Japanese had bombed Pearl Harbor, and Americans were dying overseas.

In her quiet yet commanding way, Miss Franklin began class as usual with the news. That day the news was Gretchen.

"Would you stand and tell us a bit about yourself?" Miss Franklin said.

Gretchen didn't just stand. With utmost assurance, she walked to the front of the room and faced us.

"I'm Gretchen Fay Bocher," she said for the third time. "Like *rocker* but spelled with an *h*. My family and I live on Mill Pond Road. I have five-year-old twin sisters, Carla May and Roberta Kay, named after our uncles, Carl and Robert. I was named after my grandmothers, Gretchen Majors and Fay Bocher.

"I like to write and read, but I can't sing. I don't know anything about softball. We've always lived in a city, and I'd never even seen snow before we moved to Chicago.

"We left Los Angeles right before Christmas because my father lost his job. He wrote for a newspaper. When the Hearst chain bought that paper, my father was supposed to write hate stories that called the Japanese ugly names like Nips, mad dogs, and the yellow peril. After Pearl Harbor, people were becoming afraid of all Japanese, even the American citizens. My parents and some others in our church tried to help some of the Japanese in our neighborhood. The paper fired him."

Gretchen paused. I thought she was done, but she wasn't.

"We moved to Chicago to live with Grandma Bocher, but my father could get only part-time work with a paper there. It was Grandma's idea that we move down to her cousin's farm. The house had been empty since he died."

Gretchen paused again, then smiled. "So that's how I got to Hannah," she said and sat down.

Miss Franklin nodded. "That was quite a speech." She turned to the class. "Do you have any questions?"

No one moved. Under Miss Franklin's direct gaze, no one, not even Johnny, dared to roll his eyes. A new student usually mumbled a name and maybe a place and sat down in a hurry. Gretchen was different.

* * *

It was a wonder I got anything done that morning. Half the time I was watching Bill Elliott, and the other half I was watching Gretchen. I barely managed to study my spelling list before it was time for the test.

Finally, it happened. As Bill was putting away his spelling book, the envelope fell onto the floor. Holding my breath, I watched him out of the corner of my eye. He picked up the envelope, read the valentine inside quickly, and frowned. Glancing around to see if anyone was watching him, he stuffed it under his sweater.

I missed four spelling words for the first time that year.

The morning recess bell rang. Immediately, Bill walked over to the corner bookshelves. He glanced around once again. Then he pulled the rumpled envelope from beneath his sweater and shoved it between two books.

My heart was stifled. I felt as suffocated as my beautiful valentine on that shelf. When I turned away to hide my flaming face, I saw Gretchen looking at me.

Chapter 2

"Aren't you going out, Joanna?"

Gloria was standing by my desk, coat in hand. Betty Jean was already by the door with her arms folded, her foot tapping impatiently.

"No," I said. "I'm going to work on my geography map instead. I'll go out at noon."

"Come on," Gloria said. "Johnny is quite a show today. He'll be out by the pump like always."

"The only way he knows how to be funny is to make fun of someone else," I said. "She'd have to be deaf and blind not to hear all this carrot stuff and see the handshaking."

Eyeing me suspiciously, Gloria spoke in a tone decidedly not cheerful. "What's with you? You seem awful concerned about someone you don't even know." She paused. "You looking for a new friend or something?"

"To tell the truth, I'm embarrassed. She must think we're brainless. She's so confident and proud."

"Oh, pooh," Gloria said. "You call it pride to announce to a room full of strangers that your father's been fired? And since when have you cared if Johnny or anyone else is brainless? That girl is different. She's not going to fit in here. You know that."

"She's been here only a few hours! How can I possibly know that already?" I said, my voice rising with my temper.

Ignoring my question, Gloria said, "Well, are you going out with us or not?"

I hesitated, and Gloria took that as no. With an angry flip of her blonde head, she turned and left, followed by a scowling Betty Jean. As I stared at the empty doorway, I had an uneasy feeling.

The old hot-water radiators along the wall were clanking and popping. A murmur of voices came from the side boards where Miss Franklin was helping a small group of seventh graders with percentages. Suddenly, the pale February sun broke through the gray clouds. Sunshine flooded in the tall windows and streaked across the scarred wooden floor. It shone on the blackboard behind Miss Franklin's big oak desk. I stared at the dust particles dancing in the shafts of light. I wasn't getting my map done.

I slid off my bench seat and walked to the windows. The fifth and sixth graders were on the far walks down near the ball field, playing catch and chasing each other around. The seventh and eighth grade girls were pacing up and down the front sidewalk in clusters, all the girls except Gretchen.

She was standing by the pump, surrounded by Johnny and a bunch of the older boys. Only Taylor stood apart with his hands jammed in his pockets. Some of the boys were still shaking hands, but Johnny and the Isaacsons were in a semicircle leaning toward Gretchen. With their faces close to hers, they were pulling their eyes slanted. Gretchen stood motionless, her face sheet white.

A rush of anger surged all the way from my toes. I ran from the room, right past Miss Franklin. I hit every other step and burst through the doors below.

I could hear the chanting. "Jap lover. Jap lover. Jap lover."

I raced up behind Johnny, grabbed his shoulders, and jerked him away from her.

"You moron!" I said, screaming. "Leave her alone!"

He whirled to face me, his fists doubled up. I took a quick step backward.

"What's the problem out here?" Miss Franklin shouted from the doorway.

As Johnny stepped around me, he opened his hands, raised up his palms, and said, "Not a thing, Miss Franklin. Just getting acquainted with our new classmate."

Miss Franklin frowned. "I think you'd better come inside now," she said to Johnny.

"Whatever you say," he said, smiling.

Shortly after the doors closed behind them, the clang of the bell ended recess. The crowd of boys at the pump parted, and Gretchen stepped from inside the circle. She and I walked side by side into the building. Neither of us said a word.

At noon I ate at my desk, barely tasting my cheese sandwich. No one talked to me. With my tin cup, I dipped a drink of water from the bucketful brought up from the pump by Old Henry. I left the room only long enough to dash to the restroom outside. The morning sunshine had been brief. A fine drizzle was falling, so everyone stayed inside for noon recess.

The townies who'd gone home for lunch returned about a quarter to one. The smell of wet wool filled the whole room as damp scarves, hats, and mittens steamed from the radiator tops. When Gloria and Betty Jean walked in, other kids surrounded them. There were glances at me and Gretchen, who also sat alone at her desk, and inaudible words whispered behind cupped hands.

At precisely one o'clock, Miss Franklin rapped her desk with a ruler. As students moved to their seats, two notes dropped onto mine. Instantly, I covered them with my hand since note passing wasn't allowed. My heartbeat quickened.

After Miss Franklin began our history lesson, I slipped the notes behind my propped-up book and slowly unfolded each of them. The first one was written in red crayon.

Roses are red, violets are blue,
Your face is red, her hair is too.

The second one was a crude drawing of two figures, one labeled Carrot Hair and the other Beet Face.

For the next forty-five minutes, I looked only at Miss Franklin. I concentrated on her blue eyes, straight nose, and lightly rouged cheeks. I stared at her brown hair that was pulled smoothly back into a low bun, at her white lacy collar and her navy suit. I willed my heart to slow and my face to cool.

When our history lesson ended, Miss Franklin moved to the seventh grade side of the room. We eighth graders silently worked on detailed maps of South America. I drew tiny, precise clusters of coffee beans. Using dark green, I shaded in the Amazon jungle and traced every curve of the rivers in blue. My eyes never left the map, but I felt certain that all other eyes were boring into my back.

At two forty-five, a knock on the door signaled the arrival of Mrs. Van Holt with the pink frosted cupcakes she always baked for the Valentine's Day parties at Ten Oaks. Several other mothers entered carrying small cups of redhots and napkins printed with hearts. We slid our books and papers inside our desks as the refreshments were passed out. Then the mothers sat on folding chairs to watch the distribution of the valentines.

The bottom of the box was opened carefully, and all the valentines were dumped onto Miss Franklin's desk. Two boys and two girls, who'd been chosen earlier, passed them out. For the next half an hour, we opened and read valentines. It had always been fun, something warm and friendly we did every year. But I sat, silent and alone, wondering if the messages on my desk were from people who really cared about me at all.

I looked over at Gretchen. She was sitting straight and tall with her hands in her lap. Her desk was bare. She had no valentines, not even one. My heart pounding, I stood up, walked to the bookshelf, and retrieved the valentine hidden there. By the time I walked to Gretchen's desk, everyone was staring at me.

"I didn't make this for you," I said, "but I want you to have a valentine."

The room was as quiet as death, an appropriate figure of speech since I'd no doubt committed social suicide at Ten Oaks Elementary. Returning to my seat, I looked at no one. I had a much worse problem than a red face. I was dangerously close to tears.

When the whispers began, I was positive they were all about me. With my hands folded tightly to stop their shaking, I stared at the alphabet cards tacked above the blackboard. M was a bit crooked. The corner of P was torn off. I didn't dare cry.

I looked at the first cards. A is for antelope. B is for bear. C is for cat. I was picturing the wood-block prints in the big colorful alphabet book Grandma Grey had given me for my fourth birthday. I loved that book.

D is for duck, a white duck standing in deep green vines. E is for elephant. F is for fox. G is for giraffe. H is for horse, an elegant black stallion with white feet and nose.

I wondered if the minute hand on the clock was moving.

Ibis, jaguar, kangaroo, lion, mouse. I especially liked the print of the small white mouse nibbling on a golden head of wheat. Newt, orang, pelican.

When the dismissal buzzer above the door finally sounded at three-thirty, I was on T is for turkey for the third time, and I'd managed not to shed a tear. Stuffing my valentines and arithmetic book into my satchel, I was the first to reach the cloakroom. I grabbed my coat off the hook, pulled on my galoshes, and fled the room without a thank you or a good-bye to anyone. The voices behind me faded as my feet pounded down the wooden staircase.

The little kids already on the bus were chattering loudly and fidgeting.

"Hi, Joanna," several said.

Since I didn't trust my voice, I only nodded, dropped onto my usual seat, and huddled against the bus window. Its coldness felt good against my burning face.

Within minutes, my classmates poured from the building. It was easy to spot Gloria's stylish red-plaid coat as she and Betty Jean moved off with the group who lived on the north side of town. Bill ran to catch up with them. I watched through a blur of tears that refused to be kept back any longer. They streamed down my cheeks as Bill disappeared from sight. The town kids had all the fun. They got to see each other all the time, and they even had telephones.

U is for unicorn. V is for vulture. W is for wolf.

The country kids were piling onto the bus. When Johnny Crow came down the aisle, he reached to pull off little kids' stocking caps. The hatless ones beamed. Attention from Johnny was important.

He didn't speak to me.

Gretchen, the last to climb aboard, spoke to Old Henry and smiled at the little kids in the front. When she got next to my seat, she stopped.

"I think you have a message here," she said, pointing.

On the seat lay another folded note. I considered brushing it off onto the muddy floor to be trampled into illegibility. Instead, I picked it up. Gretchen sat down next to me as if it were the most natural thing in the world to do, as if there were no other empty seats on the bus. Turning slightly away from her, I slowly unfolded the note. Inside a lopsided red heart in the unmistakable, left-handed, backward slant that his teachers had been trying to correct for years, Taylor had written, "I like what you did today."

Tears overflowed again. Hoping Gretchen wouldn't notice, I stared out the window and brushed off my cheeks.

Without warning, Old Henry shoved the gearshift into first, and the bus lurched forward. Squeals and yells surrounded us. Gretchen and I grabbed the seatback in front of us and held on. Old Henry was hitting all the potholes as he whipped around corners to leave town. When we got to the concrete county slab, I released my hold.

"The valentine's beautiful. Thank you," Gretchen said.

"That's okay. I made cards for my friends, Gloria and Betty Jean, and for Miss Franklin." I paused, then said in a rush, "And I had an extra one."

Gretchen looked at me. Feeling my cheeks getting hot again, I stared at my hands.

"He's cute, you know," she said, leaning toward me.

"Who?"

"The boy you made the valentine for."

My cheeks went from hot to flaming. Gretchen put her hand to her mouth, but I heard the giggle.

"I'm sorry," she said. "But your face is really red."

"I know." I hesitated. "I'm famous for it."

I reached into my satchel and pulled out the beet-face, carrot-hair note. Gretchen looked at it and grinned as she took a crumpled paper from her skirt pocket. Her note was identical.

"Oh, I can do better than that," I said, handing her my second note.

"No, you can't," Gretchen said.

Her grin widened as she pulled out a second note. It was the same, except for the pronouns being reversed. Suddenly, she frowned.

"I've got a problem," she said as she opened one of her books and removed the valentine from its envelope.

"What's that?" I said, my heart beating faster again.

Pointing to the blank space below the verse, she said, "If we're going to be friends, I need to know your name, especially if you're going to 'love me true' like this says."

My cheeks went from flaming to whatever color was redder than that.

"I'm sorry," she said quickly. "I was just being funny. This is a beautiful valentine, and he's a jerk for getting rid of it."

"Joanna," I said softly, staring at my hands again. "Joanna Elaine Grey."

"Well, Joanna Elaine Grey," she said, thrusting out her hand, "it's nice to meet you, and I'm honored to have this valentine."

"It's nothing," I said, shaking her hand. "The verse isn't even any good. It should be 'I love you truly.' Miss Franklin's a real fanatic about correct adverbs."

"I think I see what your problem was." Gretchen looked at the valentine and read, "Roses are red, violets are 'bluely.' You do not know, but I love you truly."

We were both laughing when Johnny said loudly from the back of the bus, "My, but Carrot and her red-faced buddy are sure having a good time. You'd hardly know there's a war going on."

Everyone got quiet. Gretchen's grin disappeared. Mine, too.

"What's the story about him?" she said in a whisper, tipping her head toward Johnny.

"He thinks he's a big shot. He used to be funny, liked to clown around and pull practical jokes."

"But now?"

"He's been different since his brother enlisted in the army last fall. Jeremiah's stationed in Alaska."

"Oh," she said quietly.

Old Henry hit the brakes several times and swung onto Mill Pond Road without slowing much. We held on.

"I think I caused you some trouble today," she said. "I'm sorry."

For the first time, I looked Gretchen directly in the face, searching for hints of sarcasm, but her large gray-green eyes were serious.

"You're sorry," I said. "You've been ridiculed or ignored all day, and you're apologizing to me. Gloria's right. You are different."

Gretchen looked away from me. Then she said, "I guess I'd better ask directly since I'm about home. Is it bad here to be different?"

No one had ever asked me a question quite like that before, so I had to think a bit before I answered. "I don't know if it's good or bad, and I can't speak for anyone except me. But as far as I'm concerned, different is just different."

Gretchen's grin returned. "Thanks," she said.

The bus turned into her lane and skidded to a stop beside the rusty mailbox. Gretchen stood up and walked down the aisle. At the door, she looked back and said to me, "Save me a seat Monday."

Then, with a quick wave and a smile at all of us, she was gone.

Old Henry backed the bus around, barely missing a water-filled ditch beside the road, and headed back south.

"Yeah, Carrot's going to need a seat Monday," Johnny said loudly. "Don't forget."

I sat very still, hoping to be invisible, trying to sort out everything that had happened.

The previous night when I was finishing my valentines, Papa had accidentally spotted the "I love you true" verse on his way to the kitchen. I'd had absolutely no intention of either Mama or Papa knowing about the secret valentine. I'd carefully hidden it from Mama by working on it only after she was knitting in the sitting room. Usually, Papa ignored my schoolwork spread out on the dining table, but not then. In one of his rare joking moods, he warned me that any love pledged on Friday, the thirteenth, was sure to be doomed.

"Remember," he said, "that even on the best of days, the course of true love does not always run easily."

"Now, Charles," Mama said, looking up from her knitting, "if you're going to quote Shakespeare, do it right. 'The course of true love never did run smooth.' It's from *Midsummer Night's Dream*, you know."

Mama was apparently more concerned about the bard's exact words than who my true love might be.

Even though Papa had smiled when he warned me, he'd been right. My valentine wasn't where I'd expected it to be. I stared at the dreary, gray landscape outside as the tears threatened to overflow again.

When the bus stopped at Johnny's house, he started down the aisle, then paused by my seat. "Hey, Beet Face," he said.

Then he glared at me and pulled his eyes slanted.

Chapter 3

I sat in miserable silence as the bus bounced down rutted roads, jerking to one stop after another. Only Taylor spoke to me.

"Happy Valentine's Day tomorrow," he said as he walked by.

I tried to smile at him.

Stopping by the front seat, Taylor held out his hand to his sister, Tessie, a tiny first grader. I watched them walk hand in hand toward the house. Even during the colorless winter, the Bensen place had a well-kept, prosperous look. Tall maple trees encircled the yard and the two-story white house with black shutters. Arrayed neatly around it were a huge barn, a corncrib, a small granary, two large machine sheds, a hen house, and a storm cellar.

Even though Old Henry sped on, that last mile seemed long. Finally, I stepped off the bus into a biting northwest wind and took several deep breaths to help settle my stomach. It was getting colder. The western sky was filled with shaggy dark-gray clouds. After checking the box for mail, I pulled up my coat collar and began the walk up our narrow lane.

Crooked hedge posts supported the fencing on both sides with barbed wire on top of the left one though it was hardly necessary to keep in the small herd of docile milk cows. Spring calving would begin in a couple of months. On the right was a field of dull brown wheat stubble.

The sharp wind made my forehead ache. I ducked my head and walked faster, holding my satchel to my chest for more protection. The deep ruts in the lane were refreezing, so I had to be careful not to stumble and fall. I was eager to get into the warm kitchen, but I wasn't eager to meet Mama.

Every day she greeted me by asking about school. However, I was never certain how much attention she paid to what I told her. I reported to her about homework and projects assigned, about students' misbehaviors and achievements, about who had on a new dress or whose brother had joined the army.

While I drank hot chocolate and talked, Mama bustled around the kitchen preparing supper. After ten minutes or so, she'd send me to my room to change into my work clothes and then list my before-supper chores, urging me not to dawdle. Right up there with cleanliness and ladylike behavior was the virtue of keeping busy.

As I approached the house that day, I considered experimenting to see if Mama did listen to me. I thought about saying, "I got mud on my hankie because Old Henry drove like a maniac, and I went outside without my coat to rinse out the spots. I stared at the new girl's fiery red hair. I didn't get an A+ on my spelling test. At recess I barely escaped having my nose bashed in. I ate lunch alone because I'm a social outcast. During the party, I made a spectacle of myself in front of everyone. I cried on the bus. And now Johnny Crow believes that I'm a traitor to my country."

If Mama said, "That's nice," I'd know once and for all that she really didn't listen to me.

With the cold biting through my coat, I hurried toward the back porch. When I opened the door into the kitchen, Mama said, "How was school today?"

I hesitated. Then common sense and a bit of fear kept me from making the confession I'd planned.

Instead, I said, "There's a new girl in the eighth grade who used to live in California. She's got twin sisters. They live in the old Herrin house on Mill Pond Road."

Mama started to peel potatoes.

"My map of South America is almost done, and we had our valentine party this afternoon. Mrs. Van Holt's cupcakes were very good."

As Mama continued preparing the potatoes, I drank my hot chocolate and, with a lump in my throat, read her some of the funny valentine cards.

Finally, I said, "It's getting colder. The sky looks like snow."

"That's nice," Mama replied. "You'd better get busy now. Remember to hang up your dress, and be sure to put on an extra sweater before you go out to feed the chickens."

At least she'd heard the part about the temperature.

* * *

It did snow that night, big fluffy flakes that piled up evenly on every surface. Saturday dawned clear and cold.

After I did breakfast dishes, I worked with Papa outside. We shoveled paths to the barn and the chicken coop. I fed and watered the chickens and the pigs and gathered the eggs. Then Papa and I started the big job, cleaning out the cow stalls.

I'd been helping Papa in the barn since I was not quite eight. The idea of her only daughter scooping manure had offended Mama's sensibilities, but I'd begged, and Papa, for once, had backed me against Mama. We won. He got me a small shovel, and I became his helper, like the son he no longer had.

My twelve-year-old brother, Cyrus, died when I was three. He got sick on an overnight camping trip with a group from church. His appendix burst before Mama and Papa got him to the hospital thirty-five miles away.

I didn't remember much about Cy even though I sometimes went to the attic to look at the snapshots Mama kept in a red velvet box. The boy in the pictures had dark straight hair like mine and a big smile. Apart from the pictures, I had only hazy memories of hearing Papa laugh and Mama laugh and Cy laugh.

I leaned into my shovel and bent my knees slightly as Papa had taught me to do. Once I was into the rhythm of a job, like scooping manure, I was free to think. My thoughts were a jumble. I doubted that I'd ever be able to look at Bill again, nor would Gloria and Betty Jean ever speak to me. Then there was Gretchen, who could giggle over notes meant to be insulting and who already knew she was different and didn't seem to mind. And

Taylor, who didn't help Gretchen at the pump but who held Tessie's hand to help her down the steps and across the yard.

Papa's voice broke into my thoughts. "Done?"

"Just about."

"Let's finish up this stall together and call it a day. I can smell your Mama's valentine cookies from here."

"That's cow poop you smell, Papa."

He frowned at me, trying to look stern, but I could see the corners of his mouth twitch. "Don't you let your mama hear you talk like that. She'll wash out your mouth and make me fire my number one helper."

We hung up our shovels and headed for the house through the flakes that were falling again. As we trudged across the snowy barn lot, I tried to picture walking beside my older brother. I wondered if Cy would've shortened his steps so I could keep up as Papa did.

Suddenly, I said, "Did Cy like me?"

Papa stopped dead and faced me, his eyes wide in surprise. "What on earth do you mean?"

I blurted out the question again before my eyes filled with tears. Papa's face softened. He put his arm around my shoulders.

"You don't remember, do you?"

I shook my head.

"Cy was hauling you around in his wagon padded with pillows before you could walk. If you were napping when he got home from school, he'd wake you up to play, which upset your mama to no end. You adored him, too." He paused, then said softly, "I was almost glad you were too little to understand when we lost him."

Papa stopped at the back steps, tipped up my chin, and said, "Does that answer your question?"

I nodded.

"Do you want to tell me why you asked?"

"No special reason."

"Well, then," he said with a grin, "let's go eat some of those cookies."

Papa didn't laugh much, but he wasn't always serious either. It was as if when Cy died, he left Mama and Papa with their decency and their caring, but he took their joy. In the eleven years that had passed since he died, I'd been unable to bring back the laughter.

* * *

The snow fell all afternoon, so Papa canceled our plans for a rare Saturday night in Hannah. He'd promised to take his "two best girls" to a movie at the Castle. Instead, we settled for popcorn and apples while Papa and I played double solitaire and Mama knitted.

Our Sunday plans were also at the mercy of the weather. Mama insisted we try to get to church despite the fact that the township's ancient snowplow hadn't cleared our road. We bundled up in extra sweaters and scarves and got one mile to a deep drift created by the Bensens' barn.

While Papa and Mr. Bensen started to dig out the car, Mama and I walked through the boot-top high snow to the house. Mama joined Mrs. Bensen, who was having a cup of tea, and I went to the barn to find Taylor. He'd just finished the milking and was pouring the last bucketful through a strainer when I walked in.

"I heard your dad outside and wondered if you were with him," he said.

"You know Mama and going to church," I said. "Unless the snow is over the top of the car, she thinks we have to try. Somehow God will forgive our not being in the pew if we're stuck in a drift instead."

"Wonder if Old Henry will make it tomorrow," Taylor said.

"I wouldn't mind if he didn't."

"That doesn't sound like you, great student that you are."

"You know what I mean."

"Yeah, I guess you don't need teasing from me, too."

"It was more than teasing, what Johnny did to Gretchen," I said. "I saw him from the window. He wasn't teasing, and she knew it."

Taylor avoided looking at me. He didn't speak as he rinsed out the milk buckets and hung them up.

"Let's go look for Mollie's new kittens. I think they're in the carriage room," he said.

I followed as he ran to an enclosure at the other end of the barn. A once-splendid black carriage sat amid cobwebs and dust. Hay from the mow above littered the floor. We listened at the doorway for a minute before hearing the tiny meows. Slowly, we tiptoed to a pile of hay nestled against the inside of a wheel. We peeked through the spokes at Mollie's four new kittens. Their eyes barely open, they crawled on wobbly legs, biting at each other's pointy tails. When Mollie scampered through the door, her back arched and her tail straight, we left immediately. Having kittens as early as February was unusual, and sometimes they didn't survive the cold. We hoped Mollie wouldn't move them from their cozy nest.

"Thanks for the note Friday," I said as we walked back. "Sorry I've been cross with you."

"Two milestones," Taylor said, grinning. "You've admitted to not wanting to go to school, and you've apologized."

"You're impossible."

We were standing face to face at the barn door, ready to go outside. I was looking straight into his brown eyes.

"I think you're as tall as I am," I said, in surprise. "You've grown."

"Sneaked up on you, didn't I?" he said, grinning again. "I've been waiting for someone to notice. I've grown almost three inches since school started. Mom's threatening to padlock the pantry. I'm hungry all the time."

I'd always been taller than Taylor. Actually, everyone in the class had been taller than he was. I wondered why I hadn't noticed he'd grown.

Papa called from the house. "We're ready to go."

Taylor and I walked through the snow. Papa and Mama were taking their leave, thanking the Bensens for the help and the tea.

"Tomorrow will be okay. You'll see," Taylor whispered when we reached the car.

* * *

Monday morning came too quickly. I stood by the mailbox, stomping my feet and waiting for Old Henry to come down the road that had finally been plowed.

Friday morning the scenery had been depressingly drab, but I'd been excited about the valentine party. The fields on Monday were an unbroken expanse of fresh sparkling snow, but my mood was gloomy. Miss Franklin would be pleased that I recognized the irony involved since that was our most recent literary term.

When the bus rattled to a stop, I climbed aboard. Taylor gave me a quick smile before I sat in my usual seat. My stomach was twisted in knots, but the trip was uneventful–until Johnny got on.

"Glad to see you're alone," Johnny said. "Carrot wants to sit by you."

"Her name is Gretchen," I said, trying to sound calm and firm.

"Is that so?" he said, sneering.

"That's so."

"I think Carrot fits her much better."

I turned, looked him hard in the face. "You can think–if you call it thinking–whatever you want. But the plain facts are that her hair is red, her name is Gretchen Fay Bocher, and she doesn't seem to care one bit that you're so preoccupied with vegetables!"

Johnny didn't reply.

Snickers came from here and there, aimed at Johnny for a change. The blush on my face was from the thrill of victory, no matter that it was a small one. I'd talked

Jonathan Alvin Crow into silence. My mood brightened considerably.

Minutes later, Gretchen bounded onto the bus. Peeking out around the edges of a Kelly green stocking cap were her fiery curls.

"Good morning, everyone," she said, her whole face alive with good humor.

"Well, if it isn't Carrot," Johnny said, his sneer intact again.

Gretchen reached up and, with one smooth, sweeping gesture, pulled off her cap, allowing all her red curls to spring free. Her arm swung down gracefully across her waist, and she bowed.

"At your service, Mr. Blackbird," she said.

Laughter rippled throughout the bus. For the second time that morning, Johnny didn't reply.

Dropping onto the seat beside me, Gretchen said, "Have you ever seen such beauty? It's like the world is covered with diamonds. Snow in Chicago was never like this." She leaned across me and peered through the window. "The drifts appear sculptured, and it looks like God painted a perfect white line on every branch."

While Gretchen continued to rave about the snow, using language and images I expected to see in a poetry book, I made two quick decisions. I decided not to share her poetic descriptions since everyone already thought she was different, and I'd give her the window seat on the way home because I was being squished.

After we got to school, I heard "carrot" a few times and "Mr. Blackbird" a lot. Once someone even mentioned my name. It didn't take long for the story of the morning bus ride to circulate.

We recited the pledge as usual. But before Miss Franklin could start the day with the news, Gretchen stood.

"May I have a minute before you begin?"

"Certainly, Gretchen," Miss Franklin said with only the arch of her right eyebrow indicating her surprise.

Gretchen walked to the front of the room and pulled a paper from her pocket.

> *I came to school on an unlucky day,*
> *But I'm so happy I'll definitely stay.*
> *I earned a nickname in record time,*
> *Made one new friend—oops, that doesn't rhyme!*
> *I got the message in your cute notes,*
> *The ones with drawings and names you wrote.*
> *Carrot Top and Beet Face we'll be for you*
> *As long as you leave us out of a stew.*
> *So on this beautiful winter day,*
> *Thanks for your welcome is what I say.*

Gretchen refolded the paper slowly. The room was hushed. When she looked up with her radiant grin, the class applauded. Both Betty Jean and Gloria turned around and smiled at me. I didn't even care if my face was beet red.

Then out of the corner of my eye, I saw Johnny glaring at Gretchen. His hands in his lap were clenched into fists.

Chapter 4

On Tuesday, Betty Jean was already in the classroom when Gretchen and I walked in. She was placing small lavender envelopes on each desk on the eighth grade side of the room. As soon as she spied us, she waved. We walked over to her.

"Here," she said, handing each of us an envelope. "Yours are special."

Gretchen looked at me, eyebrows raised.

"Her birthday is February twenty-eighth," I said. "She has a party with some of the girls every year, and Gloria and I sleep over."

"More than that this year," Betty Jean said, looking around at all the envelopes. "Everyone's invited, even the boys."

"Really?" I said.

She smiled and left to distribute the rest of the invitations.

Gloria rushed over, her cheeks pink. "A party with boys, too," she said breathlessly. "And we get to stay all night besides."

Gretchen and I ripped open our envelopes to be certain. Then we squealed with delight until we realized everyone was staring at us. Heart pounding, I turned around and nonchalantly looked toward Bill's desk. An envelope was there.

I was smiling. Everyone was smiling. Since a boy-girl party on Saturday night was an uncommon treat, the invitations were creating quite a stir. Miss Franklin had to rap her ruler more than once to get us settled down. Then the day proceeded as usual.

Miss Franklin pinned up more headlines and feature stories from several issues of *The Village Press*. We were becoming familiar with news from places far to the east like Changsha in China, Burma, the Philippines, the Malay Peninsula, Singapore, Borneo, Sumatra, Bali, and Darwin in the Northern Territory of Australia. The headlines told of both advances and retreats by the Japanese. It never seemed that anyone was winning in the Pacific. There were fewer headlines from Europe, but the most recent one, "British Lose Channel Battle," was discouraging.

The fighting seemed foreign and far away until Miss Franklin hung up "Our Defenders," a column with stories and pictures of local servicemen and women from Cane County. Miss Franklin also reminded us that on February sixteenth all male citizens between the ages of twenty and forty-four had registered at designated schools for the military draft. Other men we knew from Hannah, besides Jeremiah Crow, would be leaving for the war.

At noon recess that day, we threw on galoshes, coats, mittens, and scarves and rushed outside for snow battle. Within minutes the boundaries and the centerline were agreed upon, the troops were lined up on each side, and the snowballs began to fly. According to the rules, the soldiers on each team had to stay within the boundaries of their side. They could rush the centerline to pick off enemies up close or lob snowballs from farther back and hope they'd find targets. A death hit was between neck and knees, excluding arms and hands. The team with the most soldiers "alive" when Old Henry rang the bell won. It was a fast and furious game, which left us breathless for sure and snow-splattered if we failed to duck or dodge at precisely the right moment.

Shortly after that day's battle began, the extraordinary happened. Johnny Crow cheated. Johnny was a lot of things, most of which I didn't like, but I'd never known him to cheat.

When Seth Isaacson yelled, "Hey, Blackbird, you can't hit me," Johnny charged across the centerline, dropped the snowball in his hand, and hit Seth first in the stomach and then in the eye.

As a result, Johnny spent the next day in isolation, sitting outside the room on the stairway landing. Miss Franklin also sent a letter to his father.

After that, no one called Johnny "Mr. Blackbird" again, and "carrot" and "beet" once more became words used mostly by cooks, diners, and gardeners. Johnny's mood was sober more often than not. He was being forced to share the center ring with a new kid. Gretchen, with her ready smile and warm good humor, was being accepted in record time by the big kids and adored by the little ones on the bus.

Besides that, Johnny had a big worry. His family received word that Jeremiah was stationed at a communications post on one of the Aleutian Islands. Miss Franklin pulled down the world map and pointed to the archipelago that swept a thousand miles out into the Pacific. Only inches separated the tip from Japan. I glanced at Johnny as she pointed at the map. His face was pale, his mouth pulled tight. I almost felt sorry for him.

During recess a day or so later, I walked around the far corner of the building near the restrooms in time to see Johnny shove Gretchen against a tree.

Pulling his eyes slanted, he said, "You're a dirty, stinking Jap lover."

"Hey," I yelled, running toward them.

Johnny turned to me, his face twisted. He said through clenched teeth, "You're no better. You're a Jap lover's friend."

He shook his fist at both of us and fled behind the trees that bordered the ball field.

"Thanks," Gretchen said. "I'm all right."

I would've believed her if I hadn't seen her hands trembling.

* * *

The next Sunday when I got to church, the first thing I saw was a pew full of curly-haired redheads. The Bochers, all five of them, had come to join the United Methodist Church of Hannah. I was thrilled to see Gretchen, who slipped across the aisle to sit with me.

"We've always been Methodists," she said quietly. "I wanted to surprise you. You are surprised, aren't you?"

I knew Mama, whose cold had kept her out of the choir, would shush me if I dared even whisper, so I only smiled and squeezed her hand.

We listened to Bible readings and the choir. We sang "Onward Christian Soldiers." Actually, I sang and Gretchen hummed slightly off key. Apparently, she wasn't being modest when she'd told us she couldn't sing. Pastor Patterson's sermon was about how God would help us destroy our enemies.

"We must not despair," he said. "Truth and goodness are on our side. The heathens of Asia and those in Europe who have forgotten Him shall perish."

Every week the sermon sounded the same to me. We were right, we were the true believers, and everyone else was wrong. And it wasn't only our enemies. In our own country, other religions were wrong, or at least misguided. It bothered me. I found myself thinking a lot about how anyone could be so positive that one religion had all the answers.

I'd never expressed thoughts like that at home. Once I'd tried to talk to Pastor Patterson. He'd said it was a matter of faith in our interpretation of the Bible. That answer seemed most unhelpful since people of many faiths believed in the same Bible.

A sharp poke from Mama snapped me back to attention. I hastily bowed my head and closed my eyes as

Pastor Patterson launched into the final prayer. I asked God to forgive me for my blasphemous thoughts during Sunday worship.

After services, Pastor Patterson joyfully introduced the Bochers to the congregation and announced that there would be a get-acquainted potluck dinner in the church basement before Wednesday night's Bible study and choir practice. I loved potlucks. Our church had lots of them. Hannah wasn't short of wonderful cooks, and a bite or two of twenty different dishes was a treat–Mrs. Evans' deep-dish pie, scalloped potatoes, peas and mushrooms, deviled eggs with paprika, Mrs. Van Holt's date bars. My mouth watered.

The congregation grouped around the newcomers to welcome them to Hannah and our church. I kept smiling at Gretchen. For the first time in my life, I had a friend I could see almost every day. Taylor looked happy, too.

* * *

The following Monday I sat in shocked silence as Bill Elliott stood and said, "Today's my last day. We're moving back to Iowa."

"We're sorry to lose you, especially when you're so close to graduating," Miss Franklin said.

"Can't be helped. You know Granddad died last month. Now it's up to my dad to take over his furniture business."

"I understand," she said. "You may turn in your books at the end of the day."

I cried in the restroom all during morning recess. I cried again outside after lunch. When Old Henry rang the bell before one, I called up every ounce of courage I had, walked directly up to Bill, and slipped him a note which said, "I'd like to write you a letter. Please send me your new address when you get to Iowa. Love, Joanna."

The note didn't end up stuffed between books as the valentine had. Instead, Bill wadded it up and pitched it into the wastepaper basket. I saw him do it.

For the second time that month, I stared at the alphabet cards above the blackboard all afternoon.

Then he was gone.

* * *

On the last Saturday in February, Betty Jean had her birthday party, the same as she'd done every year since we'd started school. In the past, she'd always invited seven or eight girls for games and a white cake with pink marshmallow frosting. Afterwards, Gloria and I had stayed overnight–Gloria in the top bunk, Betty Jean in the bottom one, and I on the floor in a bedroll.

Inviting boys, serving German chocolate cake, and having Gretchen overnight as well completely broke that tradition, and, despite all the excitement the invitations had stirred at school, the party was basically a flop. First, the boys stood huddled on one side of the living room, refusing to play the games Betty Jean had planned. The girls huddled on the other side and also refused to participate since the boys wouldn't. Then several boys and most of the girls turned down the German chocolate cake.

"Nothing German for me," said Johnny, the first to refuse a huge piece though I figured chocolate's reputation for causing pimples was the real reason for his refusal.

Finally, Betty Jean turned on the radio. No one danced, but at least the sound helped fill up the silence. It was a relief when nine o'clock came, and everyone, except the four of us, went home.

We put on our flannel gowns, brushed our hair and teeth, and spread out bedrolls for Gretchen and me. Then we all climbed into our beds, fluffed our pillows, and snuggled down in the blankets to sleep.

About ten minutes later, Gloria needed another trip to the bathroom downstairs, and Gretchen wanted more chocolate cake, Betty Jean, too. I decided to hang up my good dress, which I'd tossed over a chair. Gretchen and Betty Jean returned with loads of cake and milk and leftover chicken, which we ate while we talked about actress Carole Lombard's death in a plane crash in the Nevada mountains.

At twelve, Mrs. Jones came in and said, "Girls, you'd better get some sleep."

We tried to talk in whispers. We even succeeded for awhile. We talked about the war and the Sonja Henie-John Payne movie we'd seen at the Castle and romance and boys. At first we talked about boys in general, but soon the conversation moved to Bill–I could finally mention his name without tears running down my cheeks–then to Karl, Taylor, and eventually Johnny.

"That first day at the pump," Gretchen said, "Johnny was so furious, and I didn't know what I'd done to make him mad."

"Oh, Johnny's harmless," Betty Jean said. "As a matter of fact, he used to be funny."

"Remember what he did in fifth grade?" Gloria said with a grin.

Betty Jean and I began to laugh.

"No fair," Gretchen said. "You have to tell me, too."

"All right," Gloria said. "We were lining up to go outside for recess, and Johnny voluntarily went to the end of the line instead of elbowing in or begging to cut like he usually did. Just as we got outside, there was this tremendous boom that rattled the windows. Mr. Tanner made us stay outside while he rushed back inside. A few seconds later, he opened the upstairs window and bellowed, 'Johnny Crow! Get up here!'

"A bunch of us followed Johnny upstairs. The room was filled with light gray smoke, and Mr. Tanner was pointing at the pencil sharpener, which was all twisted and mangled and hanging from one bent screw. Johnny looked really surprised. He said, 'Gee, Mr. Tanner, I didn't mean any harm. Honest. I only wanted to make some noise. It was just a teeny firecracker.'"

By the time Gloria finished the story, all of us were laughing.

Then I told Gretchen about the little newt that Karl Hoffmann had found along the banks of Red Fox Creek. He brought it to school, and we put it into an old fish tank with a tree branch, lots of muddy sand, and some water. Using Mr. Tanner's biology book, we looked up newts and salamanders to find out what they ate. Then Johnny asked how newts reproduced, and the whole class got hysterical. Reproduction, even that of a lowly amphibian, was not a topic for serious classroom discussion at Ten Oaks. Mr. Tanner ignored all the giggles and snickers and said that mud puppies were oviparous—as if that word explained it all.

That evening I looked up *oviparous* in Mama's college dictionary. Johnny must have looked it up also because the next day a huge goose egg, which dwarfed the four-inch newt, appeared in the tank. Even Mr. Tanner smiled.

"Now, Johnny," I said in a voice mimicking Mr. Tanner's, "you surely don't expect us to believe this itty bitty creature laid this great big egg."

We were laughing again.

"Then one night last winter after a snow fall," Betty Jean said, "Johnny went to the ball field and stomped out a gigantic profile of a woman with huge—"

She stopped. She was holding her fingers widespread about ten inches in front of her chest.

"Bosoms!" Gloria and I said together.

"Right," Betty Jean said. "Anyway, the lady made great viewing from the upstairs windows until Miss Franklin wondered why so many of us preferred looking outside to going outside for recess. Shortly after her discovery, we watched Old Henry and Mr. Tanner run up and down the ball field. Behind them, they were pulling a long board with a rope tied to either end, trying to erase Johnny's artwork to protect our tender minds."

After we stopped giggling, Gloria said to Gretchen, "See? Johnny can be a lot of laughs, and he likes to be the center of attention."

"I think it's more than that," I said, remembering how he'd shoved Gretchen up against the tree with no witnesses around. He hadn't done that to be the center of attention.

"What more could it be?" Gloria said.

No one answered that.

"He still scares me sometimes," Gretchen said.

Suddenly, her expression cheered. "Can you keep a secret?"

We swore we could.

Gretchen crawled out of her bedroll and went to her clothes bag. After rummaging in the bottom, she pulled out a floral-printed autograph book. She undid the little clasp and carefully turned the pastel-colored pages until she found one printed in delicate characters.

"We were friends with several Japanese-American families in Los Angeles," Gretchen said. "My dad's friend, Kenji Matsuyama, wrote this for me on my tenth birthday."

"That's Japanese?" I said, peering at it closely.

Gretchen nodded. "I used to know exactly what it said word for word, but I've forgotten now. Something about the precious gift of friendship. His daughter, Eileen, was my best friend there. She's fourteen, too."

"How did you talk to her?" Gloria said.

"What do you mean?"

"Well, you can't talk Japanese, can you?"

Gretchen laughed, an easy laugh that seemed to come from somewhere deep inside her.

"She speaks English. Eileen's American, like us. She's never even visited Japan. She was born in California up near Fresno. They moved to Los Angeles when she was seven. Her older brother, David, is in college."

"And they all speak English?" Gloria said uncertainly.

"Yes, and Mr. Matsuyama also speaks Japanese because he's *Issei*."

"What's that mean?" Betty Jean said.

"*Issei* is the Japanese word for those born in Japan. They're first generation immigrants. Mrs. Matsuyama, Eileen, and David are *Nisei*, which means they're second generation, born here."

No one spoke. Gretchen looked at us with a puzzled expression on her face.

Finally, Gloria said, "Do you have any idea how Johnny and some of the others would act if they knew you were actually friends with Japanese?"

"But why is that any different from us being friendly with the Germans who belong to the Lutheran church and farm northeast of town?" I said. "Lots of them speak German. We're at war with Germany, too."

"It's not the same thing at all," Betty Jean said, her voice rising. "We know we can trust–"

"It's two o'clock!" Mr. Jones bellowed as he pounded on the door. "Go to sleep!"

We scrambled into our beds and pulled the blankets up around our chins.

"You two," Gloria whispered, her eyes round and serious as she looked down at us from the top bunk. "I'd sure keep all of this quiet if I were you."

Betty Jean reached over to turn out the lamp. We said goodnight and drifted off to sleep.

Chapter 5

February turned into March, which was supposed to come in like a lion but go out like a lamb. Whether it was the weather or the war, there was nothing gentle about March of 1942.

After the snow melted, the temperature stayed above freezing both night and day for a few days. Then the rains came, and the country roads became deeply rutted and nearly impassable. The road commissioner declared them too soft for heavy vehicles and pulled off the buses until further notice. Those who were lucky rode to school in someone's car. I was not lucky.

The idea of gas rationing was in everyone's thoughts even though the most recent story in *The Village Press* had been headlined "Expect Gas Rationing Decision Soon."

President Roosevelt hadn't even decided, but Papa and Mama with patriotic enthusiasm were already driving less to save gasoline and wear on tires.

So every day I slogged through the mud for four miles, two of them with Taylor, to meet Old Henry at a paved road. Because Tessie's tiny legs couldn't manage the difficult walking, Mrs. Bensen was teaching her the first-grade lessons at home.

The misting rain and fog, which veiled all we could see, painted the world in shades of gray. The lifeless trees were dark silhouettes; the only sound was moisture dripping from the branches. There was nothing colorful about Red Fox Creek except its name. We didn't see the sun for days.

To add insult to injury, if we weren't at the paved road exactly when Old Henry arrived, he honked the horn while we struggled through the ruts, our boots heavy with mud.

"How come he has to do that?" I said. "He can see that we're coming as fast as we can!"

Taylor didn't complain. He trudged a little faster, throwing mud daubs up even higher on the backs of his pant legs.

Gretchen was also walking. She, however, found the whole experience to be a grand adventure–at least at first.

The changeable nature of Midwestern weather was new for her.

"Los Angeles is really a desert," she said. "A season change there means that the hillsides turn green when it rains in the winter. Here you never know what a day will be like. I can't wait to see spring and summer."

Taylor and I found her cheeriness hard to take as we cleaned up at the pump before entering the school building each day.

One morning as Old Henry pulled to a stop in front of the school, Gretchen turned around to Taylor, who was sitting alone in the seat behind us.

"Can you keep a secret?" she said in a whisper.

I'd promised to keep her secrets several times, but it was the first time Taylor had been included.

"Sure," he said.

Pulling an envelope from her coat pocket, she said quietly, "I have a letter from Eileen. Meet me at the far oak tree if we get to go out for recess."

After getting us settled down, Miss Franklin presented the morning news, which was always related to the war. The large bulletin board on the sidewall was filling up with headlines.

Enemy Troops Land on Java
West Coast Japanese Prepare for Evacuation
One Hundred Men Lost When U.S. Warship Sunk

No Rubber Available for Car Tires
Japanese Move Toward India
Yanks and Aussies Bomb Thirteen Ships
Corregidor Blasted by Japs
WPB Orders Tea Consumption Cut

Sometimes the stories were so upsetting I had difficulty concentrating on the Greek myths we were reading or on the arithmetic assignments she gave us.

At recess that day, Gretchen and I walked casually to the farthest oak tree. Taylor followed a bit later. Luckily, we attracted no attention. Taylor often made our twosome a threesome, sitting as a buffer between the boys in the back of the bus and us, doing homework with us at church in the back pew on Wednesdays during choir practice. Ever since Gloria's warning to keep quiet about having Japanese friends, Gretchen hadn't mentioned Eileen to anyone except Taylor and me.

"I've been waiting for months to hear from Eileen," Gretchen said. "I wrote her at Christmas right after we got to Chicago, and then I sent her a valentine with my address here."

"Why did it take her so long to answer?" I said.

Gretchen took the letter from the envelope and read aloud.

I didn't answer your Christmas letter because I didn't know the answers to your questions. Now I have some answers, but it makes me very sad to write them to you.

I don't know how much news about us you get back there, but on February nineteenth, President Roosevelt signed Executive Order 9066, which means we're going to have to move. Father says we must follow the government's orders to prove we're loyal to America, but I wonder what we've ever done to make anyone doubt our loyalty. Father has no answer.

Do you know we can't go into lots of stores and restaurants now? Sometimes my stomach hurts so bad when I see the "No Japs" signs that I go home and throw up. Mother, David, and I are citizens. And Father has been here since he was seventeen. How can anyone think we're enemies?

Father feels we're luckier than some of our neighbors. His boss hasn't fired him, and no one's damaged our house. Dorothy Zendo's father lost his job in January, and the Yokidas' flower shop had all of the windows broken out of it. Last week the

Kimatas' chickens were stolen from their backyard coops and killed in the street. I threw up then, too, when I saw the blood and feathers and guts smeared all around. Sometimes I'm afraid to walk where I've walked for years. I know what Father says, but I don't feel lucky.

Everyone talks about what will happen next. No one knows where we'll be sent. There are new rumors every day.

I hope I can keep writing to you. I wish you were here to make me laugh. Please write me right back. I fear we may be leaving soon.

P.S. What does falling snow feel like?

By the time Gretchen finished the letter, tears were running down her cheeks. We waited uneasily, not knowing what to do or say, while she refolded the letter and returned the envelope to her pocket. Then she blew her nose.

"The headline about Japanese evacuation that Miss Franklin put on the bulletin board, that's what Eileen is talking about," Taylor said. "I wonder what the whole story says?"

"Do you have papers from the last few weeks at home?" I said.

"I think so."

"Can you look for the story? Bring it tomorrow?"

"I'll try," he said.

The bell rang.

"Where can thousands and thousands of people be sent?" Gretchen said, more to herself than to us, as we moved toward the building.

Taylor and I had no answer.

* * *

Taylor found the story, which had come from Los Angeles. With our heads together, we read it on the bus the next morning. It said that notices were being posted throughout the communities on the West Coast informing all people of Japanese ancestry to get ready for movement to inland locations under government supervision. They were to abandon all property to Oregon, Washington, and California. They could take only what they could carry, including bed linens and blankets, dishes and silverware, extra clothing, and essential personal effects. Absolutely no pets would be allowed.

We looked at each other in shock.

"They're going to lose everything," Gretchen said.

I stared at the article, trying to imagine leaving the farm, our house, all the keepsakes Mama had stored in trunks in the attic, my doll collection and books, Grandma Grey's piano, the delicate china in the buffet, Papa's records, our old dog Jasper.

"Hey, Taylor, what are you and those girls looking at?" Johnny said loudly from the back of the bus.

"A paper," Taylor said as he quickly slipped the clipping inside his arithmetic book.

"Must be mighty interesting."

"Not especially."

"Let me see it," Johnny said in a demanding tone.

Gretchen stiffened.

At that instant, Old Henry swerved to miss a huge pothole in the road. Bodies, books, and lunch pails flew in all directions. Shrieks filled the bus. By the time we gathered our things, Johnny had forgotten the article.

We'd have to be more careful.

* * *

The unusually warm, wet weather for March continued and so did our treks through the mud. One morning Gretchen sat down on the bus seat beside me with an unusual frown on her face. Without even saying hello, she looked down at the caked layers of mud on her boots.

"I've quit cleaning them off every day," she said. "It doesn't do any good. Our back porch is a mudroom, which Mom says she may never clean up. Does this weather ever end?"

Taylor and I exchanged knowing smiles.

"Carla and Roberta can't go outside to play since they don't have boots. No one in California has rain boots. I'd have been in real trouble if Mrs. Van Holt hadn't given me this old pair."

Suddenly, the bus lurched right, then left, and back right as Old Henry tried but failed to miss a series of potholes. We grabbed the seatbacks.

"Where did he learn to drive?" said Gretchen, still frowning.

Even though she still spoke to Old Henry when getting on and off the bus, she'd complained more than once that he never spoke back.

"Old Henry was a hero in the last war," Taylor said.

"Yes, but where did he learn to drive?" Gretchen said again.

"He got the school job," I said, "because he fought in the war. I made the mistake once of complaining about his driving at home, and Papa got real upset because I'd criticized Hannah's most decorated soldier."

"Same here," said Taylor. "Old Henry returned from Europe with all sorts of medals for bravery. My folks said people wanted to help him, but it was obvious that he'd come home physically all right but mentally peculiar. He didn't talk enough to work in the bank or a store. Finally, the school board appointed him Ten Oaks janitor. He could do that job without saying much. Then a few years ago when the one-room schools closed, he became the bus driver for our part of the consolidated district."

"All that's interesting, but you still didn't tell me where he learned to drive," Gretchen said, but at least she was smiling.

As we walked toward the school, Gretchen looked at the dark, overcast sky.

"The air feels different today, kind of heavy and wet, even a little warmer. Does this mean spring?" she said.

"I wish," I said. "Probably only means more cold rain. I wonder if the bus will ever get back on the gravel roads again."

During geography class, Gretchen was the first to notice the change in the sky. When Miss Franklin asked her to name the three largest South American countries and their capitals, Gretchen was peering out the window.

"I've never seen a sky look quite that color," Gretchen said, ignoring the question.

Miss Franklin's right eyebrow shot up, but she said nothing. She walked to the west window, scanned the sky quickly, then strode across the room to the door.

"Sit quietly," Miss Franklin said. "I must leave the room."

All of us looked toward the windows. Enormous piles of heavy gray clouds were rolling toward Hannah with their undersides hanging down in ragged shreds. The sky close to the horizon had a strange, yellowish cast, and the air was still.

Dashing back into the room, Miss Franklin said in a tone that demanded obedience, "We're going to the rooms below. The fifth and sixth grades are already moving down the stairs to Miss Pensky's room. We'll join the first and second graders in their room. Each of you should crouch, as we've practiced, under a desk with a smaller child. Now go quickly and quietly."

Row by row, we filed down the staircase.

"What's happening?" Gretchen said in a whisper, her face serious.

"A storm," I said, forcing a smile. "We'll be okay."

Mrs. Schumacher already had her little ones under their desks. As we joined them, I saw lots of big arms go around small shoulders.

"Hi, Josie," I said as I joined the little girl huddled beneath the desk.

"Are you afraid?" Josie said, her brown eyes huge in her tiny pale face.

"Oh, no," I said, hugging her tightly.

I hoped that qualified as an acceptable white lie since I had too much on my mind to worry about the damage a lie would do to my immortal soul, another part of my being with which Mama was very concerned.

We didn't have long to wait. Breaking the silence, first wind and then rain slammed against the windows with ferocious strength. Almost immediately the electric lights blinked once, twice, then went out, plunging the room into darkness even though it was mid-morning. Branches crashed down outside, hitting the roof and windows. Hailstones battered the already-shuddering building. I waited for the windows to shatter and the roof to cave in. The sounds of the raging storm pressed in on me until I was struggling to breathe. My mouth was dry, but sweat was running down my cheeks, maybe tears. I needed to move from that cramped space beneath the desk. I needed air. There wasn't enough air.

I wondered if death would bring silence.

Suddenly, the tiny body next to mine began to shake.

"Are you all right? Are you hurt?" I was shouting to make myself heard.

"Mommy, Mommy," Josie sobbed.

I could barely hear her above the storm.

"We'll be all right," I said, hugging her closer. I wanted to rock her, but there was no space.

I didn't know how long we crouched like that, surrounded by blackness and the shrieking wind. Eventually, the pounding on the windows began to lessen as the hail passed, leaving only the rain, which seemed gentle in comparison. Then the wind subsided, and the building ceased to shake. I was alive, Josie was alive, and there was enough air to breathe after all.

"Children," Mrs. Schumacher said, her voice quivering a bit as she arose from behind the big desk, "you may move out from under the desks but sit quietly in the aisles while Miss Franklin and I check on the conditions outside."

I crawled out of the cramped space, unable to see much in the dim light. I dragged Josie out and held her tightly. She was trembling and sobbing with her eyes squeezed shut.

"You're safe now," I said. "The storm's over."

She didn't respond.

"Open your eyes. Look at me."

Her shaking continued.

To get her attention, I took her face gently in my hands and said firmly, "You can hear me. Now open your eyes. Talk to me."

She obeyed, but tears poured down her face. Leaning up close to my ear, she said, "I wet my pants."

I almost smiled.

"No one will notice," I whispered. "I about wet mine, too. And I'll bet we aren't the only ones."

A weak smile crept across her face. Giving a big sigh, she snuggled up against my shoulder while we waited for the teachers to return.

* * *

It was Old Henry, with finger-pointing and brief commands, who took charge, and the real surprise was that the teachers let him. Old Henry sent half a dozen older boys to neighboring houses to get buckets. One side of the roof was damaged, and water was dripping into Mr. Tanner's room in three places. The eighth grade girls were sent up there to put away any dry books and materials left on desks.

Just before I went upstairs, I tied my cardigan sweater around Josie's waist to hide the wet spot on the back of her dress.

"You were a brave girl," I said. "I'll see you later on the bus."

Her face broke into a huge smile as she hugged me.

While we worked upstairs, the teachers downstairs got the little kids into a big group to sing hand-clapping songs.

By the time we had buckets under the leaks and materials cleared away, the school board president, Mr. Cookus, had arrived. There would be no school for a couple of days due to the roof damage, he said. As soon as he got word that the main roads in the country were clear and the downed power lines everywhere were dead and therefore safe, we'd be sent home.

Meanwhile, the little kids sang themselves hoarse, and the bigger ones cleared much of the debris from the schoolyard, making large piles of branches and shingles along the edge of the street. The sky remained gloomy, but the rain had tapered off to a fine drizzle. By lunchtime, we were dirty, wet, and tired. We joined the little kids in the downstairs rooms, shared our lunches with the townies, and waited. It was another hour before Deputy Schaffer arrived to declare it safe for us to leave.

After the bus was loaded, Old Henry zigzagged out of town a different way to avoid downed trees and power lines. We saw lots of missing shingles and a few collapsed porches and garages. However, if that storm had been a tornado, the people in the part of Hannah we were seeing had been lucky.

Gretchen had been quiet since the storm, her face expressionless as she helped clean up.

"You all right?" I said as we boarded the bus.

"I've never seen nature show such fearsome power," she said.

The ride was unusually quiet as everyone stared out the windows at the damaged trees, broken power poles, and debris.

"If your family needs any help, go to Pastor Patterson," I said to Gretchen as she stood to get off the bus. "He'll know what to do."

She nodded and left without saying good-bye to anyone.

* * *

As Taylor and I began our long walk home, he was also unusually quiet. Finally, he said, "You look cold."

"I am, kind of. I don't have my sweater."

"How come?"

"Are you still good at keeping secrets?" I said, looking at him.

"Sure."

"Well, Josie McCalla had an accident during the storm, and my sweater was desperately needed to cover up the evidence."

Taylor smiled. "You're a good person," he said.

Then he was quiet again as he plodded down the muddy road.

"I'm glad Tessie wasn't there," he said at last. "I wasn't sure we were going to be all right." His voice broke. "Little kids should have the chance to grow up."

For the first time in my life, I reached over and took his hand. He let me hold it. We walked side by side, hand in hand, and I didn't feel so cold.

When the Bensen farm came into view, Taylor dropped my hand and began to run despite the mud pulling at his feet. I struggled to keep up.

"It looks fine," he said, yelling.

Mrs. Bensen and Tessie were standing on the porch, waving at us. First they hugged Taylor, then me. Mrs. Bensen fixed cups of hot tea and honey for us in the dim kitchen. She asked many questions about damage in Hannah. As Taylor described the storm, I drank my tea quickly, feeling the warmth spread through me. I was eager to get home because I knew Mama and Papa would be worried, and there'd be a lot of extra work to do.

"May I walk Joanna home before I start my chores?" Taylor said.

I glanced at him in surprise.

Mrs. Bensen hesitated. "We have a lot of work to do, with no power and all. But I suppose you'll have time before dark, and you don't have to do any homework with no school tomorrow. Your dad's already gone to check the north herd, and he won't be back until after dark. So go, but don't be too long."

"Thanks," he said.

Taylor ran to his room to get a dry jacket for himself and a sweater for me. We sat down on the porch steps to pull on our muddy boots.

"Now who's the good person?" I said as we walked back to the road.

He smiled and said nothing. As we got closer to my house, I strained to see the trees and barns in the distance.

"Your place will be all right, too," Taylor said, reading my mind as he did so often, but this time I didn't feel annoyed.

Mama didn't hear us come up. Neither did Jasper, who, though normally a good watch dog, was deathly afraid of storms and was probably still cowering in the barn. Mama was filling the kerosene lanterns on the back porch steps. When she turned and saw us, relief flooded her face. I think she would've hugged me if Taylor hadn't been there.

"Oh, you're home early," she said.

"The school roof is leaking," Taylor said. "We're supposed to stay home until Thursday."

"Anyone hurt?" Mama said.

"Not that we saw," I said, "though trees and power lines and some roofs took a beating."

"We never saw a funnel cloud," Mama said, "but the sky had that yellowish color."

She clamped her lips tight to stop their quivering. It took a lot for Mama to hide her fear of storms.

"Where's Papa?" I said.

"Out back somewhere, checking the livestock and the buildings. He's going to have to pump water by hand for the cows until he can move them down to the pasture by the creek."

"Can I help with some chores before I go back?" Taylor said.

I looked at Mama, who shrugged.

"She needs to rinse out the buckets in the barn, then pump water for the chickens and for us, too," Mama said. "You can help her if you like."

Before I had time to enjoy the idea of having Taylor's company, she turned to me. "Go change out of that dress. It certainly is a mess."

I felt my cheeks getting warm. My irritation at being scolded in front of Taylor was short-lived, however. After

I changed into my overalls and flannel shirt, Taylor and I had milk and cookies in the kitchen. Then we went outside.

It was nice to work with Taylor. We chatted while we took turns pumping water and holding the buckets. There was often silence at our house since neither Mama nor Papa talked a lot. I was sorry when Taylor said he needed to go home.

Mama and I swept the cobwebs out of the old outhouse and scrubbed off the seat with hot, soapy water.

"I can't believe your father wanted to tear this down when we got indoor plumbing," she said. "I told him you can't count on the power and the water being there all the time."

She seemed almost glad to have the opportunity to prove Papa wrong. I, however, didn't look forward to the walk out to the smelly old building, even if it was for only a few days.

For supper Mama made beef stew on the old wood cook stove in the basement. We ate by the soft light from the kerosene lanterns. After she and I heated water in buckets and did the dishes, we went to bed early, in darkness and in silence.

* * *

The stories and the headlines in *The Village Press* for the following days let us know how lucky we'd been. "North Cane County Digs Out; Five Dead" was the lead story March seventeenth. The tornadoes had barely missed Hannah, veering north a few miles. In the Midwest and the South, they'd caused devastation along a six hundred mile strip through six states–137 had died, over 1,000 had been injured, and property damage was in the millions.

For almost a week, the newspaper headlines, pictures, stories, and obituaries related to nature's ability to kill and to destroy replaced those related to mankind's ability to do the same. It was a change, but it was not a welcome one.

Chapter 6

"I can't ride with Old Henry for four more years," I said when Taylor told Gretchen and me the news. "They can't do that. They can't!"

But they had done it—and with great public support.

Mr. Bensen had attended the May school board meeting. After lengthy discussion, the board had decided to consolidate the grade school rural bus runs with those for Cane County South High School in order to save fuel and tires. Old Henry would be our driver.

Taylor and Gretchen were staring at me. I was certain my face was flaming.

"It's because of the war," Gretchen said in the patient tone she used to explain complicated ideas to her little sisters.

"We all have to do our part," Taylor said, sounding like an ad for war bonds.

I turned away from both of them, unable to speak for the lump in my throat. The tears that threatened to spill down my cheeks blurred the freshly plowed fields and green pastures sliding by the bus window.

In my head, I knew that nothing was as important as the war effort. I knew that rubber for tires was scarce and that gas rationing was in force in the East, but in my heart, I was bitterly disappointed.

It seemed impossible that a war being fought half a world away in either direction was affecting our lives every day. But it was.

It was because of the war that I hadn't gotten a new Easter dress in April. Papa and Mama had put the money for new spring clothes into war savings bonds, which were advertised everywhere. *The Village Press* had run a full-page ad showing a little girl with tears brimming in her eyes. In large print, it said, "I haven't had a letter from my daddy for two months. He's a prisoner. Help win the war and bring him home. Buy bonds."

Mama had altered my blue-flowered print dress from the previous year. She'd planned to let down the hem and add lace around the skirt to cover the crease, but to her surprise, she discovered that the bodice fit too snugly over my developing chest. So she completely remade the top as well to add the inches I needed.

"Are you all right?" Gretchen said quietly, breaking into my thoughts.

"I guess so," I said.

We were silent awhile longer.

When I was sure my voice was steady, I said, "I didn't mind not having a new dress for Easter. I was even proud to wear my old white hat with only a new blue ribbon on it."

"It looked nice," Gretchen said.

"I can handle not having many sweets," I said.

Gretchen nodded. I looked back out the window.

Sugar rationing had begun in early May, eight ounces per week for each of us. Mama had a special drawer in Papa's big rolltop desk for ration books. We baked cookies once a week instead of twice, and the jam was out only for breakfast toast. The War Production Board also asked people to cut tea drinking in half, and sometimes there wasn't coffee at the Piggly-Wiggly. The paper claimed there was no real shortage of coffee. Instead, people were over buying and hoarding it. That explanation didn't seem to make Papa any happier on the days when he had no coffee for breakfast.

Everyone was being urged to plant large vegetable gardens, even townspeople. Vacant lots in Hannah were cleared and plowed up for more space.

Also because of the war, factories that produced things like washing machines, typewriters, and vacuum cleaners quit manufacturing those goods and converted to war materials.

Then came another huge disappointment for me. No new telephones would be installed for civilians. There had been phones in Hannah for years, and I'd hoped we'd get lines out into the country. I hadn't even told Gretchen and Taylor how upset I was when we read that item in the paper.

As the bus bounced down the street in front of the school and lurched to a stop, I said, "I didn't expect the war to affect us so much."

"Me neither," Gretchen said. "And it's only the beginning."

* * *

At the same time that the war was changing our lives, the cycle of the seasons continued as if the war didn't exist at all. Shortly after the tornado, the rain had stopped, the roads dried, and spring burst into full glory. The robins returned. For days on end, the sky was cloudless and blue. The trees began to have a hazy yellow-green look as tiny leaves developed. Mama's red and yellow tulips bloomed. In fields everywhere, tractors pulled plows that turned over the black soil. The lilac bushes all around Hannah flowered, adding every shade of purple and a delicious smell. Almost over night, the grass turned bright green. Splotches of deep lavender appeared throughout the woods as the redbud trees bloomed.

Gretchen was again sitting next to the window on the bus, raving about the beauty of the Midwestern spring even though her view was dulled considerably by layers of grime. Old Henry hadn't washed the bus in months, apparently conserving water even though it seemed to be one of the few things not being rationed.

Six of Papa's Guernsey cows had calves. Gretchen, who'd never seen a birthing before, was there on the Saturday afternoon Matilda had her baby. Tears of joy ran down Gretchen's cheeks when the small damp calf licked her hand with its pale pink tongue. There were also three litters of noisy piglets in the barn and a bunch of lambs in the south pasture. Mama got a crate of day-old chicks from Fruhling's Feed Store in Hannah. Gretchen liked to sit on an overturned bucket in the chicken coop and let them peck at her shoelaces.

I was certain that once the after-school and weekend chores increased, her enthusiasm for farm life would wane. I was wrong. Gretchen enjoyed everything.

Our parents accepted our constant togetherness. We'd discovered that we were a thirty-minute bike ride apart if we zigzagged across country. It meant walking our bikes down the cow path beyond our north pasture and across a wood-plank bridge, then biking a ways on gravel before cutting across a quarter section of woods on foot, and finally riding another couple of miles on a dirt road.

Sometimes I'd get off the bus at her house to help her with chores. Gretchen often had extra jobs to do since her mother hadn't been feeling well. Mama had even taken them dishes of chicken and noodles and beef stew. I knew Gretchen was worried about her mother, but Mrs. Bocher insisted it was nothing to worry about. She promised to see a doctor.

After we'd finish the outside chores, I'd leave, riding Gretchen's bike to my house. A day or so later, she'd ride the bus to my house, help me if she could spare the time, and then ride her bike back home.

Sometimes we'd each ride our bikes to the old barn on the deserted Conrad place, which was about equidistant from our houses. Taylor, too. We'd cleaned out a corner in the tack room and little by little furnished it with old stools and crates, making it into a clubhouse, which even had a hidden niche in a wall for secret messages.

No matter what the job, Gretchen loved working outside that spring. We'd helped plant huge gardens at both places and later spent hours hand weeding tiny seedlings and hoeing the bigger vegetables.

Gretchen had to wear a huge straw hat and one of Papa's faded blue work shirts to shade her pale skin. Even so, freckles popped out across the bridge of her nose. I just tanned darker brown, even with my hat on.

We laughed and giggled and told each other secrets. I was happier than I'd ever been. And then the war would jump right back into our lives again, impossible to ignore.

* * *

For years the churches in Hannah had sponsored a party for all the graduates of the two elementary schools, Ten Oaks and Rolling Hills. It was the Lutherans' turn to host that year. The date had been set for months.

One Wednesday night in late May, Gretchen, Taylor, and I were doing our homework as usual in the back pew of the church while the adults had choir practice. Taylor was making a face each time Mrs. Yost sang flat, which was often, and I was trying hard not to laugh and catch

Mama's attention. Mama had very definite ideas about proper conduct in a church building, and they didn't include laughing at a flat soprano.

Suddenly, Mr. Evans rose and asked if he could have a word before the choir broke up into Bible study groups. "The wife and I've been thinking, and we've decided there shouldn't be an eighth grade graduation party this year," he said.

"There shouldn't?" Pastor Patterson said, looking surprised.

"Well, it doesn't seem to be the patriotic thing to do, considering the times and all."

"I don't understand," Papa said.

"It's the Lutheran church," Mr. Evans said loudly. "Those people are Germans. Their religion is German. With this war and all, we don't want to party with them."

Taylor, Gretchen, and I reached for each other's hands as the silence grew heavy. We were about to lose our party.

Finally, Mr. Bocher rose. "I'm a newcomer to your community," he said. "Maybe I shouldn't be the one to speak."

He paused and looked around. No one asked him to sit down.

"What I want to say is that if I'm going to have to hate someone in this world, I want it to be for a better reason than where he or his parents or his grandparents or even his great-grandparents were born, or what religion he's chosen, or what languages he knows how to speak. In America we have all kinds of people who have been coming here from all over the world for over three hundred years. Now if they've wanted to be part of our country badly enough to give up all their history and family in those foreign lands, I for one believe that they're Americans. I can't imagine that someone like Mr. Fruhling from the feed store is my enemy because he was born across the Atlantic and speaks German with his wife."

Mr. Bocher paused, then said, "We left California in part because of the hatred there. The Japanese we know are peaceful, hard-working people. They are not our enemies. It would be terrible to have the kind of prejudice we saw there infect this part of the country, too. Our children are losing their childhood in this bloody war. I say let them have this small celebration they've earned."

With that, he sat down.

Scarcely breathing, we waited to see what would happen. There was no vote, not even more discussion.

* * *

The party was held at the Lutheran church the first Saturday in June as planned. Taylor chose me to be his partner three times for games we played. We had a wonderful time.

Hazel Evans wasn't there.

* * *

Mama had always insisted that I establish a summertime routine the first Monday after school let out. My summer days at home were as structured as they'd been at school.

That summer Mama expected me to develop a schedule of daily chores as usual, but there were two major differences. One was fewer trips to Hannah for groceries and errands in order to conserve gasoline. That meant seeing Gloria and Betty Jean less often. The other was that Gretchen and I were allowed to do our work together, and there was more than ever with the gardens so big.

Gretchen and I worked with such enthusiasm that we often ended up with spare time in the afternoons. Sometimes we were invited to tea parties at Carla and Roberta's "very own house." It was actually a small, three-room cottage formerly occupied by a hired man. Mr. and Mrs. Bocher had scrubbed it down and furnished it with odds and ends from the attic for the girls' sixth birthday in May. Sometimes we took the girls to wade in the creek or to play with Tessie Bensen and Mollie's kittens.

Other times Taylor joined us, and we escaped from the little girls. We'd catch tadpoles in the pond or climb the huge apple tree at the Conrad place or bike for miles.

We decided to keep up with the war news the way Miss Franklin had done at school. On one wall inside the Conrad barn, we pinned up newspaper headlines and stories. Gretchen borrowed an atlas from her dad so we could locate the places we were reading about—the Aleutians where Jeremiah Crow was stationed, Moscow and Rostov in Russia, Egypt and other parts of North Africa, the Philippines, and Burma. We cut out stories about more rationing, about girls being trained as mechanics, about new draft ages, about the governor canceling the State Fair because of the transportation costs involved.

On Mother's Day, we'd read a story about a woman from the northeastern part of Cane County who had five sons in the army. For weeks the picture of her expressionless face surrounded by five framed photos of her sons in uniform haunted my dreams. I wondered if she ever slept at all.

And in June, we read that in all of California, Washington, and Oregon, there wasn't a single free Japanese person. Over 110,000 of them were imprisoned. The newspapers called it evacuation or removal. Editors must have thought those words sounded better than imprisonment.

One week later, a long-awaited letter from Eileen sadly answered the question Gretchen had asked months before.

"They're living in a horse stall," Gretchen said.

"Oh, yeah, right in the middle of Los Angeles—" Taylor said before I nudged him hard.

"They're at a race track," Gretchen said, ignoring Taylor. "They're sleeping on straw mattresses. Eileen actually saw horses being loaded into trucks as the people were arriving."

Taylor and I stared at Gretchen. She unfolded the letter and started reading from the second page.

Horses mean horse manure and horse manure means flies, more flies than I ever imagined existed. I don't know what's worse—the heat, the smell, or the flies. There are wide cracks between the floorboards, so keeping out the smell and the flies is impossible.

In the stall next to us is a young couple. Their four-month-old baby boy has colic. Mother thinks the woman's anxiety may have affected her milk. Whatever the case, he cries all the time, and I alternate between feeling sorry for him and hating him.

There's no privacy in our stall. We get dressed one at a time behind a sheet Father tacks up each morning. The bathrooms and showers are even worse. There are no partitions. Mother would think it unladylike for me to tell you about this, but it's true.

We sold all our possessions in Los Angeles, but we got little money since all the white buyers knew we had to leave. Our neighbors burned their piano and smashed their refrigerator rather than take the ten dollars offered for them. Father didn't fight in that way.

David wasn't allowed to finish the semester at the university. He's very bitter. Father still insists that we mustn't fight the government. He and David barely speak.

Mother cries when Father is not in the stall.

I keep wondering if the rest of the country knows what's happening to us. I'm keeping a diary and drawing pictures of the racetrack. Mother says I shouldn't want to remember this, but somehow I think I should remember. Besides, what else have I got to do except that and write to you?

As Gretchen refolded the letter, Taylor and I were silent. We didn't know what to say.

* * *

What was frustrating was that, except for the Bochers, few people around Hannah did know what was happening out West. Fewer yet seemed to care.

One Sunday after church, I overheard Mr. Evans say to Papa, "It's a good idea to pen up all those Japs out there in the West. For their own protection, you understand. It's safer for them to be separated from the families of all our boys fighting in the Pacific."

"Well, I'm not sure," Papa said.

"Personally, I'd ship them right back to Japan. You can't tell what kind of sabotage they're planning," Mr. Evans said.

Stepping up close to Papa, I said, "But what about the ones who are American citizens?"

Mr. Evans' eyebrows shot up. His jaw tightened. "And what do you know about–"

"Joanna," Papa said, "your mother wants you."

I looked toward her. "No, she–"

"Go join your mother," Papa said firmly.

As I walked away, Mr. Evans said, "These youngsters. Imagine trusting slant-eyed Nips."

The knot in my stomach made it hard for me to swallow Mama's Sunday dinner of fried chicken and fresh peas.

Chapter 7

A couple of days later, Taylor showed up before the dew was off the grass. I was hanging bed sheets on the clothesline.

"You're up early," he said as he grabbed one set of corners to help me.

"How'd you get away this time of day?" I said as I spaced four clothespins evenly on the sheet. "We're not going to check on the raspberry bushes until this afternoon."

"Mom said I could come. I can't go with you this afternoon."

"Why not? Gretchen's coming. It's all planned."

"I have to leave after lunch," Taylor said. "That's what I came to tell you."

I turned suddenly, dropping a pillowcase back into the basket.

"Leave? Why?"

"My Uncle Howard, who lives near Robinson, was hurt in an accident. He fell fixing the barn roof. He has cows, and my cousin Lawrence can't do all the milking alone."

"So you need to help?"

Taylor nodded. "Dad said he could spare me since the crops are planted and the first cultivating is done. I'm catching the bus this afternoon."

"How long will you be gone?"

"I won't be back until school starts."

"That's all summer," I said in disbelief.

Taylor stood there staring at me. I felt my face getting warm.

"I love the way you look right now," he said quietly.

He stepped close to me, put his hands on the sides of my face, and kissed me gently on the lips. Then he slipped an envelope into my hand and walked away. As I stared after him, he stopped at the corner of the house and smiled the way he'd been smiling at me since we were toddlers. Only never before had my heart beat so fast.

I stood rooted to that spot with the sheets snapping in the wind behind me. Then I looked at the pale blue envelope in my hand. Leaving the rest of the wet wash unhung, I dashed into the house.

"I need a hankie," I said to Mama as I rushed up the stairs.

With the door closed behind me, I stood before the mirror, staring at what Taylor had seen. Wind-blown strands of hair had escaped from the blue scarf I'd tied around my head. My developing bust and hips, slight though they might be, weren't even visible beneath my long loose shirt. I looked positively plain, not at all beautiful or glamorous like the movie stars, especially since Mama absolutely forbid the use of lipstick or rouge or even a bit of powder until I was sixteen. The longer I looked the more certain I was that Taylor Bensen was in bad need of glasses.

I sat down on the edge of my bed and opened the envelope.

> *Dear Joanna,*
>
> *I guess by the time you read this you'll know if I had the nerve to show you how I feel about you. In case I didn't, I want to say that I'd consider going halfway across the state to work for my uncle a grand adventure except that I wanted to spend*

the summer with you. Gretchen, too, but especially you.

Will you write me? I've enclosed my uncle's address. I want to know what you're doing and thinking and feeling. And keep me posted about Eileen. How can people be expected to live in horse stalls? Have you thought about writing to Eileen, sort of like a pen pal? It could cheer her up. You might ask Gretchen what she thinks. I know that letters from you will cheer me up.

I'd like to be more than

Your friend,
Taylor

I read the note several more times before Mama knocked on my door. Heart pounding, I slipped the envelope beneath my mattress.

"The next load's ready to hang," she said.

"I'm coming."

As I walked through the kitchen, Mama said, eyeing me carefully, "Are you all right? You look flushed."

"I'm fine, Mama. Just fine."

* * *

About three o'clock, I left on my bike to meet Gretchen. I saw her coming before I got to the old Conrad place. She was riding much faster than usual down the bumpy lane while waving one arm in the air. She skidded to a stop in front of me.

"I have the most wonderful news," she said breathlessly.

"I have news too, but—"

"Mom went to the doctor. She's not sick. She's pregnant. We're going to have a baby!"

Gretchen dropped her bike, twirled around a few times, and plopped down in the tall grass. I stared at her in surprise.

"It's a boy. We're sure it'll be a boy," she said exuberantly.

"How can you be sure?" I said.

"The odds. We have three girls, so we're due for a boy."

"And your mother really wants to have another baby, even with a war going on?"

"Oh, yes. A war doesn't change the way Mom and Dad feel about each other. Dad says that Mom's pregnancy shows we have faith in the future."

I was quiet. I couldn't imagine a new baby at our house, war or no war. Nor could I imagine my parents doing what couples do to make a baby. I'd seen animals together. I knew basically what had to happen between a man and a woman.

Once I'd asked Mama why I didn't have a little brother or sister, back when I still believed that doctors brought babies in the black bags they carried. Mama had said there were reasons. When I got older, I'd assumed she meant she and Papa didn't love each other that way any more.

The Bochers were different. They touched each other and laughed easily. Sometimes I'd see them walking hand in hand, checking the garden or going down the lane to get the mail. The Bensens were like that too, easygoing and affectionate with each other. Not Mama and Papa. I'd never seen them kiss or even hold hands.

"Is something wrong?" Gretchen said. "Aren't you happy about the baby?"

"Sure I'm happy," I said with more cheerfulness than I felt. "It's that I have some news, too, and mine isn't so good."

"Oh, what news?"

"Taylor's gone."

"We saw him yesterday. How can he be gone?" Gretchen said.

"His uncle got hurt, so he's taken the bus to Robinson to work the rest of the summer."

"We're really going to miss him, aren't we?" Gretchen said, dismayed.

"Yes," I said, looking down to hide my pink cheeks.

We got back onto our bikes and headed down the lane toward the raspberry patch. Beyond the old barn, we laid the bikes down and trekked through the tall grass. As we walked around the area, I pointed out the fullness of the berries that were beginning to turn a rosy color and predicted a bumper crop in July. Gretchen and I would no doubt spend a lot of time there, dropping berries into small buckets hanging from our necks on cords. It was a loathsome chore since it required wearing heavy clothing in the hottest weather. To make it even worse, Mama would douse our ankles and wrists with smelly kerosene and tie our pants and shirts there to prevent chiggers from crawling up our arms and legs and boring into our skin.

The only saving grace would be the delicious cobblers and jam Mama would make, but with sugar rationed, I wondered how much we'd get. At least we'd have plenty of fresh raspberries sprinkled with a bit of sugar and covered with fresh cream.

I talked to Gretchen about writing Eileen, and she was enthusiastic.

"When did you think of it?" she said.

"It was Taylor's idea," I said.

* * *

That night when I wrote Taylor the first time, I suggested he write Eileen, too. And so began a summer of letter writing–until Mama walked down to the mailbox one day and saw a letter from Eileen.

"Matsuyama?" she said, looking at the name and return address on the letter. "Who's Eileen Matsuyama?"

"She's Gretchen's friend in California."

"What's she got to do with you?" Mama said.

"Nothing. She's feeling lonesome, having to leave her home and all, so I write letters like a pen pal."

"She's Japanese."

"No, she's American."

Mama pointed to the name. "Matsuyama–that's not American."

"Don't you start, too," I said loudly, feeling the color come into my cheeks. "Eileen is just a girl, an American girl like me. I try to cheer her up."

"Don't you raise your voice with me, young lady. You aren't old enough to know how this would look to people in town."

"I thought you and Papa supported Mr. Bocher," I said, growing angry. "I thought you agreed that the Germans here aren't our enemies. Why is Eileen any different?"

"The Japanese are different," Mama said. "We don't know about the Japanese."

"Well, the Bochers do," I said more loudly than I'd intended.

Mama paused. "You won't bring suspicion on us by corresponding with this girl," she said firmly. "Is that understood?"

I glared at her, but I said no more.

That night when I picked up my pen, the tears that hadn't come that afternoon during the argument with Mama flowed.

> *Dear Taylor,*
>
> *Will you send the enclosed letter to Eileen when you write her? I've asked her to write me when she writes Gretchen. Do you think she'll even want to keep in touch with me now that she can't send any more letters to my address? I'm so ashamed.*

When I included the letter to Eileen in the envelope addressed to Taylor, I was willfully disobeying my mother for the first time in my life. Even though I was positive I was right, it didn't feel so good.

* * *

The summer heat struck with a vengeance, ripening the raspberries but otherwise making life miserable. Besides fighting the ongoing battle with the weeds, Gretchen and I were also hauling buckets of water from the pumps to rows of parched green beans and tomato plants. We were up at dawn each morning, working furiously before the heat came at midday, then trying to find ways to survive the long afternoons when the breeze dropped and the humidity rose in hazy curtains. Anxiously, we watched the western sky, hoping for rain to settle the dust, to water the plants, and to give us a night cool enough for uninterrupted sleep. Occasionally storms came, bringing strong winds, brilliant flashes of forked lightning, and rain that beat down on the crops, seemingly intent on pounding them to the ground.

Taylor's letters were filled with descriptions of work on the dairy farm. He continued to sign his letters "Hoping to be more than your friend." I opted to sign mine "As ever," even though I wasn't feeling as I'd ever felt. Days that brought a letter from Taylor were much brighter than days that didn't.

Gretchen was consumed with thoughts about the baby. One afternoon when I stepped onto their porch, she grabbed my hand and pulled me toward the front door.

"You've got to see J.L.'s room," she said.

"J.L.?"

"Joshua Lowell, our grandfathers' names. Isn't that perfect? I'm named for our grandmothers, and he'll be named for our grandfathers."

Gretchen led me down the upstairs hall toward a tiny room, which had been used for sewing. Fresh paint on the woodwork and new wallpaper–a cheerful print of fluffy sheep running through a meadow filled with colorful flowers–had transformed it into a nursery.

"Why do you suppose your parents didn't have another baby after you?" Gretchen said as we looked at diapers and gowns in the Sears catalog.

"I asked Mama once and she said there were reasons."

"Well, what reasons?"

"You know," I said.

"Know what?"

"You have to do it to make a baby."

"So?"

"Well, my parents aren't like yours."

I stopped, feeling my face getting warm.

"I don't get what you mean," Gretchen said.

"My parents, they don't love each other like yours do."

"Of course your parents love each other. They work together, go to church together. They do everything together, including sleeping, just like my parents do."

"But they never touch each other," I said.

"They're probably more private. Your mother doesn't touch you much, right? But you know she loves you."

I didn't answer. I'd have to think about that.

* * *

Summer crept on, one hot, muggy day after the other.

The war raged on as well. The wall in the barn was plastered with stories from *The Village Press*, stories about battle sites all over the world.

One evening Gretchen and I were sitting on the branches near the top of an apple tree in their orchard, hoping to find a stray breeze.

"I got a letter from Eileen yesterday. She is so depressed," Gretchen said.

"Things aren't any better?" I said.

"Actually worse. It's over one hundred every day with sand blowing through all the cracks. They have to stand in line to eat or use the bathroom or buy a stamp or do anything. People get too hot. Last week a pregnant lady in a stall near them lost her baby because she dehydrated."

"That's awful. Is Eileen okay? And her family?" I said.

"They aren't sick, but her brother is very angry. Mr. Matsuyama still insists they should be loyal to America, but David says he can't feel loyalty to people who've put them behind barbed wire and guard them with loaded guns."

We didn't talk for awhile. I tried to picture living in a stall in our barn, but I couldn't.

The only humorous thing Eileen ever wrote about was their houseplants. Alfalfa seeds from the horses' hay sprouted beneath the flooring and grew right through the cracks between the boards and into the stall. Even though Gretchen and I had laughed as we read that part of Eileen's letter, when I pictured it later, it didn't seem very funny.

* * *

One afternoon a couple of days later, I was sitting on the back steps, rubbing Jasper's ears and trying to get up enough energy in the blistering heat to take the wash off the line, when Mama stepped outside with a jar of lemonade.

"I'm taking your father a drink," she said, tying on her straw hat. "He wants to finish cutting out the corn and weeds in the north bean field before supper time."

"I can take it to him," I said.

"No, thanks," she said. "I'll go. The walk will do me good. Will you get in the rest of the wash?"

After the clothes were folded and put away, I got on my bike and headed down the path toward the pasture. Gretchen and I had decided to meet at the pond for a change. It meant a longer walk since there was no path to it, but it also meant a cooler time since we intended to get wet, clothes and all.

I left my bike propped against a fence post and skirted the edge of the pasture.

It was when I got to the trees on the far side that I saw Mama and Papa in the distance. They were beneath the shade of a cottonwood tree in the middle of the field. Their hats lay on the ground beside the lemonade jar. They were standing shoulder to shoulder with their arms draped around each other's waists. Papa was pointing toward a distant field.

Then Papa turned to face Mama. Reaching up, he removed the pins that held her hair in place, letting it unwind. He touched it gently. Then he kissed her.

Turning away, I sank down behind the trees, tears of joy in my eyes. My parents loved each other.

* * *

Toward the end of August, Mama and I were snapping the last of the green beans for canning. We were chatting about the Bochers' baby, and I described the redecorated room. That reminded Mama of how she and Papa had spent hours with the catalog choosing exactly the right paper for Cy's room before he was born.

"Why didn't you and Papa have another baby after me?" I said.

At first Mama stared at me in surprise. Then she said, "I guess you're old enough to understand now, aren't you?"

I nodded.

She poured a large bowl of snapped beans into the water in the sink and began to slosh them around. Then she took a deep breath.

"I was in bed many months during my pregnancies with both Cyrus and you. Actually, the doctor had advised me not to have another baby after Cyrus, but I seemed so strong and healthy during the years he was little that we decided to have a little girl to make the perfect family. Your father chose your name the minute we were certain you were on the way. I secretly chose the name Richard Todd in case you turned out to be a boy. I didn't tell him that until after you were born. He never once doubted that you were going to be his little girl."

She smiled at me, but it was a sad smile. "We didn't get to have our perfect little family very long."

Mama stopped washing the beans and stared at her hands. I thought she might not finish, but then she looked up and continued.

"The doctor warned me not to have a third child. He said I could lose my health, or worse. So we use birth control. Do you know what that means?"

I nodded while I focused on the pile of beans in front of me. I was remembering the book Gloria, Betty Jean, and I had found last summer hidden inside a hatbox on Mrs. Jones' top shelf.

"Does that answer your question?"

"Yes," I said without looking up.

"Then we should see to getting these beans done," she said, quickly returning to the efficient, no-nonsense mother I'd always known.

But as I watched her pour the beans into the jars and place them inside the pressure cooker, I pictured her standing by Papa, her beautiful dark hair hanging loosely down her back.

Chapter 8

About the time we thought we couldn't stand one more day of muggy heat or another sweaty night of sticking to the sheets, a thunderstorm raced through the area. The next day the air was crystal clear, the haze gone, the breeze gentle and dry. Overnight the creek widened from a trickle to a gurgling flow. The corn leaves rustled as the moisture gradually left them, and the silks on each ear shriveled and dried. Mama's sad, droopy zinnias in the front bed revived and burst into a final, glorious bloom.

Papa's thoughts turned to harvest, Mama's to fall cleaning, and mine to high school.

Mama and I had already spent several days checking over my clothes, altering some old things and boxing up others to give to the church mission. Cousin Kay's annual box of hand-me-downs had arrived, and I was relieved to see that she still had decent taste. Between what Mama could salvage from last year and what came from Kay, I had most of what would be my high school wardrobe. Our shopping trip to Hannah supplied me with underwear and socks, two white blouses, a pair of brown loafers, a blue sweater, and material for a black watch plaid jumper. Considering the way the war was going, I felt lucky to get that.

The latest news was grim. Across the Atlantic, the Nazis were in Russia, France, the Netherlands, Poland, Italy, and North Africa. In the Pacific, the war raged in the Solomon Islands and in areas near Australia.

In this country, six German saboteurs had been electrocuted in the United States on August eighth. They'd come on German U-boats to burn and blast vital American war installations. Four had landed in Florida and four on Long Island, New York.

As I waited for Gretchen in the Conrad barn one afternoon, I stared at their pictures on the front page of *The Village Press*. I tried to see them as evil, but all I saw were men who looked no different from our friends and neighbors. I wondered if they'd ever climbed trees when they were kids or fallen in love or had children. I wondered if they were sorry they'd tried to hurt Americans or if they hated us right to the end.

Gretchen saw it as terribly ironic that Japanese people in America, like the Matsuyamas, were imprisoned behind barbed wire fences when German nationals ended up being the saboteurs.

I walked to the doorway and looked down the lane. Then I sat down on a crate inside, impatiently fingering the large sealed envelope in my lap. I wanted to open it so badly.

Suddenly, Gretchen ran through the door, waving an envelope like mine.

"Sorry I'm late," she said, breathless. "Carla and Roberta insisted on three stories before their quiet time. Mother was already lying down, so I gave in to keep the peace."

"Are you ready now?" I said.

"On three," she said.

We counted, then ripped open the envelopes containing our high school schedules.

"Oh, no," I said. "I have two hours of Zimmermann."

"What's the problem with Zimmermann—he or she?"

"It's Mrs. Zimmermann. She's so strict. She expects every single written paper to be perfect. I knew we'd have her for English—every kid at Cane South for the past fifty years has had her for English—but I have her for Latin, too."

"She can't be that bad, or she couldn't keep her job," said Gretchen in an irritatingly calm tone.

"Everyone says that even the board members are afraid of her since they've been in her classes. No one would dare fire Zimmermann."

Gretchen laughed. "Now you don't believe that. She's probably a very good teacher who expects a lot from her students."

"You'll see," I said. "You have her for third hour, too."

The rest of our class schedules were about what we'd expected. I had English, geography, algebra, Latin, biology, physical education, and glee club. Gretchen and I had English and algebra together. I hoped I had some classes with Taylor, too.

Taylor's last letter was brief, five sentences actually.

There's news from Eileen. It's not good. I'll give you her last letter when I see you at the park on Labor Day. I've pictured you all summer with your hair tied back in the blue scarf. Will you wear the blue scarf for me?

* * *

In past years, Labor Day weekend was the time of Hannah's street carnival. That year the town council decided that such a celebration would be inappropriate because of the war.

Instead, on Saturday there'd be a farmers' market and a scrap drive. President Roosevelt was urging Americans to collect anything metal that could be recycled into machinery and weapons. Mr. Bocher, who turned out to be a genius at getting people to donate time and energy, had volunteered to head the drive in Hannah.

The market was to provide extra end-of-the-season produce to anyone who needed it, all donations going to the Red Cross. Mama and I had already dug up some late potatoes, onions, and turnips, and we picked the rest of the acorn squash and enough tomatoes to fill two bushel-baskets. Since I'd spent the whole summer working in the garden, it seemed strange to see it so bare.

Monday there'd be a community potluck dinner in the park followed by games and an evening ice cream social. It wasn't the celebration we'd always had before, but I was looking forward to being in Hannah for three days and to seeing friends I hadn't seen much all summer.

* * *

"You need to go to the pond to cut some cattails for Mrs. Van Horn," Mama said early Saturday morning. "I promised her some last spring. We'll take them into Hannah today. Hurry, now."

"How many?"

"Oh, two dozen or so. I need a few for Grandma Grey's old jug, too."

"Need help with the dishes first?" I said.

"No, the vegetables have to be at the park by ten, so you go ahead."

That was luck. Very little in my life ever got put before helping Mama with the dishes.

I grabbed Papa's old flannel shirt from a nail on the back porch and slipped on my dirty gardening shoes. I got a spare pocketknife out of the tool cabinet and stuffed a pair of heavy gloves into my back pocket.

It was a perfect morning for a walk. The sky was deep blue with only tiny wisps of high clouds. The gentle breeze was cool, and the sun was warm on my back. It would be hot by afternoon but a pleasant kind of hot.

The leaves on the soybeans were beginning to show a hint of yellow. Later they'd be golden, then rusty colored, and finally a pale brown. Then right before the combines started the harvest, most of the leaves would drop, revealing straight, bare stems and bulging pods.

When I got to the pond, I walked around the edge to survey the cattail stand. There were lots of them. However, the ones closest to the banks were not well developed due to a dry spell in August. I'd have to go out into the water to get the best ones.

Carefully, I waded in, feeling how slippery the bottom was even with my shoes on. I moved slowly and deliberately toward a group of perfectly formed cattails. I was almost there when my left foot slid on a moss-covered rock and my right one tripped over a submerged willow branch. My hands flew forward in a vain attempt to catch myself. With a resounding splash, my whole body hit the shallow water. Dirty water splattered all over me as mud oozed up through my fingers.

"Damn it!" I yelled, figuring that God would certainly understand my aggravation and that Mama, who wouldn't, was well out of earshot.

I rolled over into a sitting position, my eyes squished shut as the muddy water ran down my face. I was just about to say that word again when I realized that I wasn't alone. Something had rustled in the weeds near the bank. Quickly, I rubbed my wet shirt across my eyes and opened them. There stood Taylor, a wide grin on his face.

"My, what language we've learned this summer," he said.

"Don't you dare laugh at me!"

I flung a handful of water in his general direction but only succeeded in splashing myself more.

"Temper, temper," he said. "Aren't you even a little bit glad to see me?"

I was a whole lot more than a little bit glad. He looked great, taller and slimmer, dark hair shining in the sun. And the smile on his face was all for me. My heart was beating furiously.

"You'll never know," I said. "And if you even think about telling me you like the way I look, I'll splash your new shirt but good."

"That's my Joanna," he said. "Tender and ladylike."

He laughed as I struggled to a standing position and made a useless attempt to wipe the muddy water off my face. Hands on my hips, I glared at him.

"Sorry I laughed," he said, trying to hold his lips straight.

More water dripped off my face. I kept staring at him, completely at a loss for words.

"Your mother thought you'd be glad to see me," he said, still trying to look serious, "but I guess not."

Backing away from the edge of the water, he held his hands up in mock surrender and said, "Okay. I'm leaving."

I heard him laughing as he headed down the path.

Smiling, I quickly cut the cattails and raced toward home.

* * *

When Mama and I arrived at the park a bit late for the market, my blue scarf was tied around my freshly shampooed hair.

Taylor helped us unload the vegetables and carry them to the tables set up along the street. Then after he dropped by about five more times, Mama said I could go with him to find some of our friends. But instead, we left the park and walked away from the crowd.

"You have a letter from Eileen," I said.

"It's bad," Taylor said. "Several people died recently from dehydration, and some got sick from the food that spoiled in the heat. It takes hours for everyone to get through the lines for each meal."

"You know what's sad," I said. "She keeps apologizing to Gretchen for being depressed."

"How else could she feel?" he said.

Taylor took my hand, and we walked along in silence.

"It's not fair, is it?" I said finally.

"What?"

"That I feel so happy when Eileen is so miserable."

"And why are you so happy?" he said, smiling at me.

"You know," I said, right before he kissed me.

* * *

The dust cloud inching along on the far road was visible minutes before I could see the faint yellow of the bus. Despite my having dressed in my favorite skirt and my brand new blouse, I was a nervous, sweaty-palmed wreck. I felt completely unprepared to start high school. It was a huge brick building with unknown teachers in rooms scattered all over two floors, and it would be filled with unfamiliar kids who'd gone to grade schools large and small all over the southern half of Cane County.

And one familiar kid, Johnny Crow. I hadn't seen him since the graduation party at the Lutheran church, but I'd thought about him since reading the story about Jeremiah in *The Village Press*. In June, Japanese forces had begun an assault on the Aleutian Islands. No one knew exactly where Jeremiah was stationed, but when the islands of Kiska and Attu fell into Japanese hands, the letters from Jeremiah had stopped coming.

I couldn't imagine going about my daily routine not knowing about my brother, always wondering where he was and how he was, fearing that he might be tortured or starving, trying not to consider that he might not be alive at all.

The rattle of Old Henry's bus as it charged toward me broke into my thoughts. It came to a noisy, shuddering stop in a choking curtain of dust. The door swung open, and I climbed aboard.

"Hi," I said.

Old Henry didn't speak.

"Joanna," Taylor said as he tipped his head toward a vacant seat in front of him.

Our previous seating arrangement had been changed. The back seats were filled with only upperclassmen. We freshmen were sitting in the middle, where a year ago I'd sat alone.

"Are you ready?" Taylor said as the bus roared on.

"I can't believe I've been looking forward to starting high school for months," I said. "I think I'm sick."

"Dad tried to make me feel better this morning by telling me his first-day-of-school survival story," Taylor said.

"What happened to him?"

"A bunch of older guys in his gym class put him into a trashcan. He was small for his age. Then they hauled him out to the sports equipment shed near the football field."

"That's awful."

"It gets worse. Since the shed had barn doors that slid open, they stacked concrete blocks at the ends to keep them closed. Dad got out of the trash can, but no one heard him yell. So he had to stay in there three hours until the football coach came to practice."

"Did your dad get in trouble?"

"No, he was the victim."

"What about the other guys?"

"That's the funny part. Dad didn't know them, and he couldn't identify them because they'd knocked off his glasses before they put the lid on the trashcan. But the guys didn't know that. They thought he was doing them a favor, protecting them on purpose. Dad ended up sort of like their mascot, and no one picked on him the rest of the year."

"And that story is supposed to make you feel better?" I said.

Taylor smiled, though it was a weak smile.

"Any more news about Jeremiah Crow?" I said.

"Dad saw Mr. Crow day before yesterday. He says they won't give up hope Jeremiah's safe."

"Wonder what Johnny will be like," I said.

Johnny was already standing beside the road when the bus stopped.

"Hi, Johnny," the little kids in front said as he climbed on.

Johnny was taller and broader, and his hair was bleached almost white by the sun. His mouth smiled, but his eyes didn't. He seemed to fill the aisle as he swept past us. Without hesitating, he sat down among the upperclassmen in the rear.

I looked at Taylor, eyebrows raised. He shrugged.

When the bus stopped at the Bochers' house, Johnny stood up to get a better view. "My, my, if we don't have ourselves a whole garden of carrots out there," he said with a sneer.

The laughter from the back of the bus was loud and long. I felt the heat rushing into my face.

"Let it go," Taylor said quietly behind me. "Gretchen can handle it."

But Gretchen didn't have to handle it—at least not then. She was too busy helping Carla and Roberta, whose tiny identical faces were pale and serious. It was their first day of school.

"Girls, meet Old Henry, our driver," Gretchen said.

"Hello, Old Henry," they said.

After she ushered the little girls into a front seat, she turned and waved at everyone. "Hey, Joanna," she called back to me, "I'm going to sit up here with them today."

"That's the girl I was telling you about," Johnny said.

I didn't have the nerve to turn around to see who was sitting with Johnny.

When the bus stopped at Ten Oaks to unload the elementary students, Gretchen helped the twins get off. Then she moved back to my seat. More high-school students from Hannah boarded. Gloria and Betty Jean joined us, and everyone began talking at once about schedules and the teachers whose reputations had preceded them.

Even being surrounded by the cheerful chatter didn't help. My palms were sweaty, my stomach rolled, and my face was hot.

When we got off the bus at the front of Cane County South High School, we were immediately swallowed up in the swarm of students from the other buses. We moved up the broad cement steps to three sets of double doors. Once inside, the older kids split into two groups moving toward the corridors at the left and the right.

Standing on chairs around the edges of the spacious lobby were some students wearing green armbands. Each one held a sign for last names, grouped alphabetically.

"Freshmen, go to your group," one boy said through a megaphone.

Gretchen and Taylor walked away together. Gloria and Betty Jean went in opposite directions. Alone, I cautiously moved toward my sign. The boy continued to yell as more kids streamed in. A bell rang loudly, and the lobby became empty except for the hushed huddles of freshmen.

"I'm Claire," the girl holding the E-I sign said. "I'll be your guide this week. I'm going to take you to your lockers, then your homeroom where you'll get a map. I'll also answer questions. Are there any now?"

No one spoke.

"All right, follow me."

In the crowded hallway, we walked behind her, single file, weaving through the bodies like baby ducklings following their mother through a field of tall grass. A second bell rang, and the hubbub increased as students tossed stuff into their lockers and rushed into the open doorways along the hall. Claire stopped in front of a group of lockers.

"Check your schedule for your number. Your lockers have been assigned alphabetically in this area. You'll get your locks in homeroom. Follow me."

Obediently, we filed behind her again until she stopped before an open door.

"Your homeroom," she said cheerfully though my churning stomach made me wonder if she'd led us to a pond full of alligators instead. "Mr. Downers will take over now. I'll meet you in the lobby each morning this week to answer questions. Bye, now."

With a wave of her hand, she was gone.

From there the day was a blur. Mr. Downers, without looking at us, passed out building maps and locks and said "uh" so often that I began counting.

"Odd-numbered 100 uh rooms on the uh east end of the first uh floor, even-numbered ones uh on the west, odd-numbered uh 200 rooms on the east uh end of the second floor, uh even-numbered on the uh west."

That was clear enough.

Mr. McNeal was a pot-bellied, balding man with a food-spotted red tie. He paced back and forth across the front of the room, stopping only long enough to jab at various colored patches on the world map, which hung behind his desk.

"We'll study how the geography of a country is related to its role in the war, starting with the countries bordering the Mediterranean."

Mr. Bainbridge, the algebra teacher, was young, handsome, single, and serious. He assigned pages seven and eight, all fifty problems.

Mrs. Zimmermann looked as stern as her reputation. Gray hair slicked back into a tight bun, plain gray dress with no collar and no jewelry, rimless glasses down on the end of her nose. The class was quiet before the bell even rang. Gretchen turned around, looked at me, and grimaced. And I had to be there for two classes in a row.

Lunch finally came.

"Over here," Gloria said.

She, Betty Jean, and Gretchen were already sitting at a table on the far side of the lunchroom. I was glad to see them. The assigned seating in each room had kept me from talking to anyone all morning. After we ate, we huddled closely together and ventured around the lunchroom, stopping to visit other clusters of girls. My heartbeat quickened when I spotted Taylor on the opposite side of the room, surrounded by boys. I wondered if he'd seen me. I wanted to talk to him, but there seemed to be an invisible line drawn across the room with all the girls on one side and all the boys on the other. I'd have to see Taylor later.

Johnny Crow was already holding court. He was standing in the center of a group of boys exactly as he'd done at Ten Oaks. The only thing missing was the pump.

After lunch I had biology with Mrs. Anders, who told us about the class in a soft musical voice that didn't fit the gory nature of the dissection projects we'd be completing. That class wasn't for the squeamish.

Gym was mostly freshman girls. A shrill whistle and barked commands from Miss Krupinski got us into a straight, alphabetical-order line in record time. A uniform was issued, an awful one-piece gray thing which had to be freshly laundered and ironed each weekend even though it would be stored in a smelly locker room all week. Miss Krupinski's voice reverberated in the gym as she described the class activities–calisthenics, laps, health lectures, and competitive sports.

Finally, I had glee club with Mr. Carrigan, who greeted us all with handshakes and a warm smile. I was definitely ready to see someone smile.

When the dismissal bell sounded, students poured from the rooms. The slam of locker doors was deafening. Amid the jostling crowd, I made my way back toward the lobby. As I rounded the corner, I saw Gretchen near the doors. I hurried to catch up. Suddenly, Johnny and two of the older boys who'd ridden our bus appeared. One stepped forward and shoved Gretchen's elbow from behind. Her books flew everywhere.

"Watch where you're going," the boy said as he walked out.

Johnny and the other boy stepped over her books and followed him. Before going down the steps, Johnny turned back toward Gretchen, a smug look of triumph on his face.

"You all right?" I said, rushing up to help her gather the books.

"Sure," she said. "It was an accident."

"I know you think I'm gloom and doom, but don't trust Johnny or those guys."

"They'll stop if I ignore them," she said.

"I hope you're right, but I'd be careful all the same."

On the bus, I listened to the chatter. Taylor was stuck in a junior-senior gym class. Gretchen loved her French teacher but was positive her world history teacher hated kids. Gloria was already in love with the "cutest senior you've ever seen." It didn't seem to matter to her that she didn't even know his name. And Betty Jean oozed excitement. She loved everything about high school.

All I felt was exhausted.

* * *

"It's Friday," Gretchen said as she dropped onto the seat beside me. "We've finished our first week of high school."

"I've already done enough math and Latin homework to fill a month," I said, moaning. "And alphabetical order. In every class I'm surrounded by *G*s. It's Gooch, Grabanski, or Gressmore on the left and Gronwald,

Gruber, or Gudauskas on the right. Do you suppose I'll sit beside these same people for the next four years?"

"You get worked up over the oddest things," Gretchen said. Then she leaned over and whispered in my ear. "You could marry Taylor Bensen with a *B*, and then you'd get to sit nearer me."

I felt the color rising in my face.

"Beet face," she said, then giggled.

"Carrot top," I said back, trying not to smile.

"Hush, you two," Taylor said from the seat behind us. "You don't want Johnny to hear you."

We laughed. I wasn't about to tell Taylor what was so funny or why my face was red.

Chapter 9

The first frost came early that fall. Within weeks, the harvest was in full swing with the soybean fields almost bare and corn picking well under way. The trees were turning, each one flaming and burning with its own glorious shade of orange, gold, or rust. Gretchen was sitting by the bus window and describing the scenery with poetic imagery again. She was no longer certain that spring was the most beautiful season of the year.

One morning in October, I knew something was wrong as soon as she got on the bus. Her smile was missing.

"A letter?" I said.

She nodded and handed it to me. We'd been expecting to hear from Eileen ever since the last note telling us that people were being taken from the racetrack–whole trainloads taken to places they'd never been.

I unfolded the letter. It was short.

> *We've arrived. Six hundred people on our train and more come every day or so. For two days and nights, we rode with the shades pulled down and armed soldiers in each car. We're in Wyoming at a place called Heart Mountain. It sounds pretty, but it's not. The land is flat and treeless, covered only with sagebrush and buffalo grass. Heart Mountain, which is northeast of us, is a rocky, squared-off peak, not tree-covered and snow-capped like I've always pictured mountains.*
>
> *Our camp is made up of rows and rows of ugly black barracks and surrounded by barbed wire fences. We have one room, twenty by twenty-four feet, Father says. Sometimes I'm angry with myself for feeling happy that we have a room bigger than a stall. Why should I feel happy to be in a barracks? Only a few months ago we owned a house, a car, and furniture, and I*

> *had a room all to myself and privacy in the bathroom and Mother's good food.*
>
> *I want to hear about high school. We don't have school. Please write soon.*

I refolded the letter and put it back into the envelope. Gretchen opened her algebra book and slipped the envelope inside. She turned around to Taylor.

"How do you do problem ten, page forty-six?" Gretchen said, handing him the book.

"Taylor doesn't have all the brains around here," Johnny said loudly from the seat behind Taylor's. "I'll show you how to do it."

Leaning over the seat, Johnny grabbed for the book. Taylor tried to hold on, but in the scuffle the book flew open, and the letter fell to the floor. Johnny snatched it up.

"Is this a love letter?" he said.

"Give it back," Gretchen said.

"Matsuyama," Johnny said, his eyes wide as he read the envelope.

Standing up, he waved the letter in the air. His face was twisted with anger. "Hey, boys, the Jap lover has a letter from Matsuyama."

Gretchen rose. Her eyes flashed. "Give it back," she said slowly through clenched teeth.

Suddenly, the bus slammed to a stop. Lunch boxes and books flew everywhere. We grabbed for seatbacks. Old Henry rose quickly from his seat, becoming straighter and taller than I'd ever seen him before. He strode down the aisle. No one spoke, no one moved. He stopped by Johnny's seat.

"Give it back," Old Henry said.

Johnny hesitated a second too long. An old hand darted out, gripped his wrist, and pulled his arm behind his back. Johnny yelped.

"Now," Old Henry said.

With his free hand, Johnny returned the letter to Gretchen. Old Henry released Johnny's wrist. Small and stooped, he shuffled back to his seat and drove on.

* * *

A few days later someone painted a broad yellow streak down the full length of locker 138. Mr. Greerson, the principal, investigated. No one was caught. The janitor tried to remove the paint, but a faint tinge of yellow remained on Gretchen's locker.

* * *

"I really hate to see it end," Gretchen said as she looked out the bus window at the few remaining dark leaves clinging to the branches.

Autumn was over. The landscape had returned to shades of gray and brown. The harvested fields were covered with bean stubble and broken corn stalks or plowed into straight dark furrows. Pasture grasses had faded, the flowers were gone. Even the evergreens appeared colorless.

The ever-present war was also ugly. Abroad, the Nazis were battling the Russians at the Volga and Stalingrad. The British were bombing Italy, and Rommel was leading the Axis troops in North Africa. In the Pacific, men were fighting and dying in the Solomon Islands and on Guadalcanal.

At home, Kathleen Fitzhenry's family buried their eldest son, killed when his aircraft carrier was lost in the Pacific. The Crows still waited for news about Jeremiah. Gloria's cousin lay in a hospital on the West Coast, alive but blind, and the Isaacsons' uncle came home without a leg. So much sadness, so much pain.

Pastor Patterson's sermons continued to urge us to pray for victory and to sacrifice for the good of the country. And that we were doing. All extra-curricular activities and sporting events were canceled at the high school to save transportation costs. Several senior boys had left school to enlist since the draft age was being lowered to eighteen. To save both gasoline and tires, rationing plans forced civilians to drive less—no more than 5,000 miles per year—and more slowly. There were blackout practices, even in the Midwest. Another scrap drive organized by Mr. Bocher met the million-pound goal for Cane County. Women and kids had helped with the harvest even more than usual since so many farm hands had gone to war.

And because of the travel restrictions, Grandma Grey wouldn't be coming for her annual winter vacation. I'd have to celebrate my birthday in January without her for the first time since I was born.

About the time my spirits would drop, Gretchen would receive a letter from Eileen, and I'd be jolted into realizing what real hardship was all about.

I could visualize Heart Mountain. It had been built in only two months and housed 10,000 Japanese. It was the third largest city in the whole state—if a place with 450 crudely-built, tar-paper covered barracks on dirt streets with mess halls instead of kitchens, latrines instead of private bathrooms, and barbed wire fences, elevated guard towers, and high-beam searchlights should be called a city at all.

If I happened to grumble about high school being all study and no play, I thought of Eileen who was crammed into a barracks with two hundred kids of all ages. They sat at rough tables on long, backless benches with no curtains, no decorations, no blackboards, no drinking fountains, and few books.

The winds, snow, and frigid temperatures had started in Wyoming in late September. The Matsuyamas' room had a pot-bellied stove, which warmed only a circle around it. When there was a coal shortage, they let the fire go out at night. Some mornings the room was covered with a white dusting of snow that had blown through the knotholes and cracks in the uninsulated walls and floor during the night.

What I found so amazing about Eileen's letters was a lack of fury. She was being held a prisoner in her own country. In one letter to Gretchen, she wrote,

> *I can't figure out who to be angry with.*
> *It can't be Americans because I'm American.*
> *Most of us here are Americans. It can't be*
> *white Americans because that would include*
> *you and others who've been kind to us. The*
> *government? The war? Who's responsible?*
> *I may not know who's done this to us, but*
> *I'll never forget.*

* * *

One cold, rainy afternoon in early November, we were on the bus in front of Ten Oaks, waiting for the high school students who lived in town to get off the bus and for the little kids who lived in the country to get on. I'd learned early in the semester to do homework every spare minute I could find. My queasy stomach and Old Henry's erratic driving kept me from working while the bus was moving, but I often got out an assignment at the stop in Hannah.

When Old Henry rammed the bus into first gear, I grabbed for the seat back with one hand and hung onto my biology book with the other.

"Do you think God has a sense of humor?" I said.

Gretchen's eyebrow flew up. "What on earth do you mean?"

"Nothing," I said.

"No fair," she said grinning. "You can't stop after springing an idea like that."

I hesitated.

"Come on. Talk," she said.

"Well, consider animals," I said, reopening my biology book and pointing to the phyla of the animal kingdom. "All these are animals, yet they are found everywhere in every size and shape and color. All of them get food, reproduce, and survive in countless ways."

"I know that," said Gretchen. "I don't get the sense of humor part."

"Take egg laying, for example," I said. "It's simple enough. Eggs from the female need to be fertilized by the male. They incubate and hatch. Presto, babies."

"I've got that much," Gretchen said.

"It's the diversity. All the animals could do it the same way, but they don't. Some eggs are fertilized before they are laid and some after. Some are protected in nests, some buried, some laid in water, some left on the open ground. Some are incubated and protected by adults. Others are abandoned. It's like God is trying to think of every possible way to achieve egg-laying reproduction, and when we think we've seen it all, He slips in something funny like babies being born from the tummy of a male."

"What male?" Gretchen said.

"The seahorse. Mrs. Anders told us that the female lays the eggs in a pouch in the male's abdomen. He fertilizes the eggs, then keeps them in the pouch until they hatch and pop out of the opening—itty-bitty copies of the adult seahorse."

Gretchen giggled.

"What's so funny?"

"I'll bet Mom would let Dad do that for her about now."

That sent us into gales of laughter as we tried to picture Mr. Bocher with his back swayed, thirty pounds heavier, slowly dropping into a chair and needing help to get back out of it. J.L. Bocher was due any day.

We rode on in silence. Gretchen never told me if she thought God had a sense of humor, but I was amazed by the diversity in nature. As I stared out the window, I wondered if God was saddened that His most complex organisms seemed intent on destroying themselves in war. It made me sad.

"You ready?" Gretchen said, breaking into my thoughts.

"Sure," I said, gathering up my satchel as Old Henry skidded to a stop.

It was a special treat for me, a midweek overnight with Gretchen. Granted, we'd promised to study for midterms all evening, but it was a treat all the same.

As we stepped off the bus with Roberta and Carla, Johnny yelled through an open window, "There must be some kind of vegetable convention here tonight. Or maybe a traitors' party."

Gretchen ignored him. I ignored him. Taylor avoided him. But Johnny's conduct hadn't changed. Gretchen never knew when her books would go flying out of her hands or when someone would drop her homework paper as it was being passed up an aisle and then step on it with a muddy shoe before it got to the teacher.

"What's a vegetable convention?" Carla asked, taking Gretchen's hand.

"Oh, Johnny's being silly," Gretchen said as she lifted the mail from the box with her other hand. "He knows vegetables don't have big meetings. People have conventions like the one Daddy went to in Chicago."

"That was a convention," Carla said positively.

Gretchen grinned at me over the little girls' heads as we started toward the house.

We hung our coats on hooks in the entryway closet and entered the big dining room which was dominated by a heavy round oak table and a huge brightly-colored braided rug. Mrs. Bocher was sitting in an easy chair near the windows, hemming a tiny baby gown.

"Have a good day?" she said as the twins flew over to her, both talking at once.

"We'll start supper," Gretchen said as she laid the mail down on the table.

I chopped onions while she put hamburger into a large kettle. She opened jars of tomatoes and tomato juice we'd helped to can the previous summer and a large can of kidney beans. In a short time, the chili was bubbling, and we started peeling potatoes. The Bochers were the only people I knew who ate mashed potatoes in their chili. After the bowls were filled, Mr. Bocher placed a dollop of mashed potatoes in the middle like a white mountain rising from a lumpy red sea. Each twin made a spoon-sized crater in the top of the mountain and added a dab of butter in the center. Chili was one of the highlights of visiting the Bochers.

Another was the conversation. That night the dinner time conversation bounced around the table with the little girls repeating their school stories to their father and Gretchen explaining what we needed to cover during our midterm review after supper.

Before we were excused, Mr. Bocher held up a letter and said, "I have news to share."

There was silence.

"It's from Kenji. They're terribly cold in Wyoming. It's even colder there than here," he said, looking at the little girls.

"That's cold," Roberta said with a shiver.

"Their room is so poorly heated that on the coldest days, they sit in a circle around the stove all day, wrapped in blankets. He worries that Eileen is falling behind in her studies. The school barracks is also poorly heated as well as overcrowded and ill equipped.

"On the bright side, Kenji writes that, except for his nagging cough, none of the Matsuyamas have been ill like some of their neighbors. And the really good news is that David is going to college."

"Where?" Mrs. Bocher said.

"It's the University of Wyoming. The administration is accepting some camp residents, and the WRA is allowing some young people to leave. As for Eileen, a high school is under construction."

That was good news, indeed. There hadn't been any from Heart Mountain before then.

Chapter 10

"I need a break," said Gretchen as she stood up from the bed where we'd been sprawled, books and papers scattered around us. "Let's get a snack."

It was Friday, February twelfth, 1943, and I was spending the weekend with the Bochers.

We tiptoed down the hallway and the stairs, then ran past Mr. Bocher and Pastor Patterson, who were still seated at the dining table, so deep in conversation they didn't look at us. Gretchen went to the bathroom. As I got out some cookies and poured two glasses of milk, I overheard the men talking.

"The goal of the American Friends Service Committee, the AFSC, is to settle young families in areas away from the coasts, especially the West Coast, where people feel threatened," Mr. Bocher said.

"Like the Midwest," Pastor Patterson replied.

"Right. The editorials in the Chicago paper have helped. They've questioned the legality and morality of imprisoning an entire group of citizens without trials, even during wartime. Quite a few communities are becoming receptive to the idea of resettlement. Some are pursuing it as a way of righting an injustice."

When I heard "resettlement," my heart skipped a beat. I stepped closer to the doorway.

"I suppose the other advantage of rural areas is the need for farm workers," Pastor Patterson said.

"True. But don't let me paint too rosy a picture. Prejudice isn't only a West Coast phenomenon. It'll take–"

"Your turn," Gretchen said, coming into the kitchen.

I jumped away from the door.

After I used the bathroom, we took our snack upstairs. Heart pounding, I waited for Gretchen to tell me more about the resettlement the men were discussing. She must've heard them as well.

When she picked up her pencil instead, I said, "Your dad and Pastor Patterson are really deep in conversation."

Nodding, she said, "Aren't they always," and went back to work.

Disappointed, I reopened my algebra book. I didn't know how else to bring up the subject short of confessing that I'd eavesdropped, and I didn't want to do that. Even though my pencil moved, I kept thinking about Eileen.

* * *

The next evening the rhythmic creak-creak-pause-creak-creak-pause-creak-creak-pause of the old rocking chair was the only sound in the room. Three-month-old J.L. lay sleeping in my arms, his tiny body warm against my chest. Gretchen was lying across her bed, silently studying the wood-block pictures in my alphabet book. Outside huge wet snowflakes fell on the window and slid down the glass, leaving crooked watery trails. I snuggled into the feather pillows behind my back and let the peace of the moment sink into my heart.

Exactly a year had passed since that disastrous Valentine's Day party at Ten Oaks. Bill Elliott was a blur in my memory, replaced by Taylor Bensen, and Gretchen had become the best friend I ever expected to have.

High school was no longer a strange, scary place. I'd learned to memorize Latin, manage algebra, find every battle site on a world globe, handle Mrs. Zimmermann's unrelenting criticism of my writing, dissect an earthworm, take a shower in a crowded locker room without turning beet red, and sing four-part harmony a cappella.

J.L. stirred in his sleep. His eyelids fluttered, and his little mouth puckered as he made sucking sounds. I watched his perfect face, then kissed his forehead. Since the day he was born, the Bochers had shared J.L. with me as if I were one more big sister.

"Are you positive you want to give away your book?" Gretchen said as she gazed at the black and white zebra with one hoof raised.

"I'm certain," I said, smiling. It had taken me months to think of the perfect gift for J.L.

"You know," she said, "the girls will insist on sharing this. They're so proud of knowing the alphabet."

"That makes the gift doubly good."

"You're a true friend, even if you do blush all the time."

I made a face at her and grinned.

"Remember the party a year ago?" she said.

"I was just thinking about it. In a single day, I challenged the class bully, got snubbed by my secret love, became a social outcast, and met my best friend."

"I remember the look on your face when I sat down by you on the bus," she said. "There's no way I'd become your best friend yet."

We laughed.

"Do you ever feel guilty for being so happy when the war is going on?" I said, looking down at J.L.

"It's not exactly guilt," Gretchen said. "I'm afraid of being too happy. I think I should hide my feelings or maybe something awful will happen to even things up."

"That's what I mean," I said. "Think of Kathleen's brother. And Jeremiah Crow, wherever he is. And Eileen, imprisoned behind barbed wire and guarded by soldiers with loaded guns."

"Dad and I talked about that the night after J.L. was born. He asked what I thought the world would gain by my feeling guilty. He says that rather than feeling bad about feeling good, we should use our energy to help others."

I rocked a while. Then I said, "Is that what your dad is doing with Pastor Patterson?"

Gretchen looked so surprised I wished I hadn't spoken.

"How do you know?" she said.

"I didn't mean to eavesdrop," I said, tears welling up in my eyes.

"It's okay," she said.

I swallowed. "Last night when we went downstairs, I heard your father mention resettlement. I knew he meant people from the camps."

"Oh," she said.

The creak-creak-pause of the rocking chair filled the silence.

"I guess I can tell you," Gretchen said finally. "I don't know everything. Just that Dad met some people with the American Friends Service Committee in Chicago. They're Quakers. Dad's talking to Pastor Patterson about the church sponsoring a family here the same way we sponsor mission work away from here."

"You mean Eileen might get to come?" I said, excited.

"That's what I hoped, too, but Dad says no. Kenji is *Issei*, not a citizen, and David's in college, so their chance of getting out isn't good."

"Then who?"

"They haven't gotten that far. Pastor Patterson still has to present the idea to the congregation. There's a lot to be decided."

"I think it's a wonderful idea," I said, smiling.

J.L. squirmed. One eye opened a slit.

"You getting hungry?" I said.

His little mouth tightened into a pout, and his forehead wrinkled. J.L. could go from contented cherub to wailing baby in a short time. We headed for the kitchen to warm his bottle.

"I don't purposely keep secrets from you," Gretchen said as she sprinkled milk on her wrist to see if it was the right temperature. "It's that Dad doesn't want rumors to start before he and Pastor Patterson present the facts to the congregation."

"You can count on me. I won't say anything to anyone."

J.L. was finishing the bottle when the door flew open and the twins rushed in.

"It was wonderful," Carla said so loudly that J.L. startled.

"Mickey Mouse can dance," Roberta said even more loudly.

Mr. and Mrs. Bocher had taken them to see *Fantasia* for a Valentine's Day treat. I watched them dance around with Mrs. Bocher, re-enacting the sorcerer-broom scene. J.L., fed, burped, and diapered, was lying on my lap happily staring at his own fists as they waved in front of his face. Gretchen and her dad were in the kitchen, heating up some leftover ham for sandwiches. Once more the feeling of deep peace settled over me.

* * *

During the sermon the next day, my mind didn't wander even once as I waited for Pastor Patterson to present the resettlement idea. When he didn't, I was disappointed, but I didn't say anything, not even to Gretchen.

After services Gretchen and I hugged and wished each other happy Valentine's Day. As I headed toward our car, Taylor walked up, slipped a small package into my hand, and continued on by without saying a word. I unwrapped the tissue paper and opened the box. Inside was a delicate, heart-shaped necklace with a tiny card that said, "From Taylor, who is still hoping to be more than your friend."

"Taylor," I said.

He turned around and walked back to me.

"You are," I said.

I blushed, as I always did, but he did, too.

* * *

The blower fan on the old coal furnace rattled and squeaked as it vainly tried to force enough heat through the big floor registers to warm the church. It was a frigid, record-setting thirteen below zero that Sunday in March, and the thirty-fourth snowfall of the winter lay on the ground. Even my heavy, fur-lined boots and wool coat were not keeping out the penetrating cold. The members of the congregation sat stiffly like large carved figures—the only signs of life being the little clouds of whitish vapor that appeared before their faces with each breath exhaled.

A shivering Roberta was cuddled beneath my left arm. Gretchen sat on my right, holding a well bundled, sleeping J.L. Carla, who was also asleep, leaned on her other arm. Our parents were in the choir loft, looking fat and lumpy in their maroon robes, which they wore over their coats.

I was so engrossed in my physical misery and the irreverent thought that the entire Methodist congregation looked like cigarette-puffing chain smokers that I was unaware that Pastor Patterson had quit preaching about the need to sacrifice. All of a sudden, the words "a special mission project" jumped into my consciousness, and I was listening to him intently, even before Gretchen elbowed me.

"We support missions in faraway places," he said, "where people are poor and suffering. Now there are church congregations who are helping an especially unfortunate group of people right here in this country.

"As you know, there are whole families imprisoned behind barbed wire in desolate places in the West. These people are being held without benefit of trials. Some, who were born in Japan, have lived and worked in this country most of their lives, yet they've been prevented from becoming American citizens by our own laws. Most of the people in the camps, however, are American citizens like us.

"There are the elderly and women and children imprisoned, even babies from orphanages, all suspected of disloyalty because they look like our enemy. Their homes, businesses, and personal possessions are gone. They're living in crude buildings with only the barest necessities provided. They've lost their jobs, their dignity, their freedom, and in some cases, their health. Yet there's no evidence of disloyalty or sabotage among these people.

"Throughout history, Christians have come to the aid of fellow human beings in need. These imprisoned people are in desperate need. Right here in Hannah, in a small way, we can help right this terrible wrong. We, as a church, can sponsor a Japanese-American family. We can free them from imprisonment, bring them here, and help them get a fresh start.

"Arthur Bocher and his family have agreed to let a family live and work on their farm. We in this congregation can help by supplying them with furniture, clothing, and food until they become self-supporting members of the community. Most importantly, we can welcome them into our church.

"Next Wednesday before choir practice, Arthur and I will answer as best we can any questions you may have. As always, the final decision will be made by the five members of the missions committee.

"I ask you to pray for guidance. Search your souls for love to give to these victims of this terrible war. Please bow your heads."

Pastor Patterson's impassioned plea hung in the momentary silence. With my heart pounding, I prayed for the project. I vowed not to let my mind wander during his sermons even if he did preach on the same topic every single week forever. I begged for the project to be accepted by our church.

As the prayer continued, I opened one eye to sneak a look at Gretchen and caught her smiling at me.

* * *

I was ready for immediate action, but it didn't happen that way. Events took place with frustrating slowness.

First, there was the meeting on Wednesday night. The church was packed. Pastor Patterson began by repeating what he'd said Sunday for the benefit of those who hadn't braved the cold and come to church.

Then Mr. Bocher spoke briefly, giving information about the activities of the War Relocation Authority. He read parts of Kenji Matsuyama's letters, which described the living conditions at Heart Mountain. Mr. Bocher also pointed out that many people in Cane County had German ancestry, yet they were not imprisoned, nor was their loyalty suspect. Only the Japanese were considered to be a threat.

As it turned out, only one person voiced objections during the meeting. Wayne Evans. Mr. Bocher carefully answered each point he made. I marveled at Mr. Bocher's ability to speak. There were some questions, mostly about where the family would live and what work they'd do. There was concern about the size of the family, about not getting too many mouths for the church to feed.

Finally, the meeting ended, and the wait for the mission committee's decision began. People rose, some moving toward the door to leave. No one lingered to visit, and the church seemed unusually quiet to me. The Bochers and Pastor Patterson, however, were joyfully optimistic.

But not Mama.

After supper one evening, I was studying at the dining room table, Mama was knitting, and Papa was reading the newspaper aloud. A front-page story told about the

Japanese amassing troops on island bases near Australia. General MacArthur warned that the forces were huge.

Suddenly Mama interrupted Papa. "It's one thing to send money to help someone," she said. "It's quite another to move strangers into a community."

Putting down the paper, Papa said, "I assume you're talking about the church project."

"Of course," she said. "It may be the Christian thing to do, but I wonder how deep the Christian spirit goes with some people in the church."

"Julia, I'm surprised at you. No one except Wayne Evans has objected. How can you be so pessimistic?"

"Pastor Patterson and Mr. Bocher appealed to people's logic and intelligence," Mama said. "Who on earth is willing to speak out and appear foolish?"

"The plan is logical. It is the right thing to do. So what's there to worry about?"

"Hate and fear aren't logical," Mama said. "And I think a lot of people have those feelings about the Japanese. Who'll admit them? Especially in church and in front of others. Besides, this isn't only a church project."

"Of course, it is."

"No, Charles. The church will be sponsoring and donating, but this family will live in the whole community. The Methodist church represents part of the community but not all of it."

Papa sat in his chair, staring at Mama. "I truly hope you're wrong."

I blinked my eyes to clear the tears.

* * *

If Johnny Crow was any indication of what others were feeling, Mama wasn't wrong.

Shortly after the church missions committee voted to support the project and sent a letter to the AFSC in Chicago, Johnny and his cohorts approached Kathleen Fitzhenry during lunchtime.

"You heard what Carrot Top Bocher's going to be doing soon?" he said in a loud voice.

I felt Gretchen stiffen beside me. Kathleen sat silently, her hands clasped before her. She didn't look at Johnny.

"She's going to be helping some Japs," Johnny said. "Your brother lies dead in the cemetery, and she's going to be living with Japs."

We heard Kathleen's sobs as her head dropped onto her arms. Her shoulders shook.

Gretchen rushed to her. "Oh, Kathleen, I'm sorry. It's not like he says."

When Gretchen put her hand on Kathleen's shoulder, Kathleen jerked away. With tears streaming down her cheeks, she stared hard at Gretchen. Then she fled from the lunchroom.

Gretchen whirled around and stepped up to Johnny. Her eyes flashed angrily.

"You don't get it, do you?" she said through tight lips. "I'll explain it to you one more time."

Johnny stepped back. Gretchen stepped forward, still right in his face.

"My friend was born here, just like you. She's an American. She had no more to do with Michael Fitzhenry's death than you did. She isn't the reason Jeremiah is—"

"Leave him out of this," Johnny screamed. "Don't you ever let his name come from your traitor lips again!"

Gretchen jerked back as if he'd hit her. Tears flooded her eyes. The color drained from her cheeks. Johnny stood before her, clenching and unclenching his fists.

Suddenly, the dismissal bell clanged.

"Got to go to class," one of the boys said to Johnny. "Let it go."

Slowly, Johnny turned to leave. Then he stopped. "There's always later," he said, his back to us.

Gretchen and I stood as everyone filed out. Then I took her hand and led her from the lunchroom.

During the days that followed, Gretchen was unusually quiet. Her mother thought she was coming down with something. I begged Gretchen to tell her father about Johnny, but she refused.

"Johnny isn't everyone. He's a single angry person. There's no reason to tell Dad," she said.

That didn't make me feel much better, and I waited for something awful to happen at school.

* * *

The thirty-fourth snowfall turned out to be the last one. As the bitter cold of March gave way to the warmth of April, spring burst forth. The farmers went back to their fields, and the hum of tractors working in the distance could be heard day and night. Every day brought more warmth, more color, less fear.

Johnny's threat faded from my mind.

J.L. was a cheerful, healthy baby. We celebrated each step of his growing–when he rolled over and when he sat up, his first tooth, his first smiles, his funny habit of wrinkling up his nose and breathing really fast as if he were an animal getting ready to attack. We forgave his habit of using his new teeth to bite an unsuspecting shoulder from time to time, and we avoided his tiny fingers, which became easily entangled in hair. Best of all, J.L. still liked to be rocked.

The Bochers were busier than ever. After lots of persuasion, including Mr. Bocher's promise to build them a tree house, Roberta and Carla agreed to give up their playhouse for the family that would be coming. The little house was thoroughly scrubbed again. The kitchen walls were repainted white, and the pump at the sink got a new coat of bright red. Mrs. Bocher made red-and-white-checked gingham curtains for the windows while some church members collected odds and ends of furniture, dishes, kitchen utensils, and linens.

The Bochers were doubling the size of their garden in preparation for the new family. Already tiny lettuce leaves and onion tops were sprouting through the ground. Our garden would be huge again, too.

So much seemed right that spring. Even though the war raged, it felt far away. The Bochers' optimism continued to infect me, despite what Mama said at home. After all, I couldn't stop the war, but I was doing what I could to help those affected by it.

But then there was Johnny Crow, who had a way of darkening the brightest day. About the time I'd get all the worries shoved out of my mind, Johnny would do something to remind me that there was still plenty of hate in our lives.

After the lunchroom incident, I'd waited fearfully for something to happen. When it didn't, I decided that Gretchen was right. I worried too much.

Then I saw her frown one day as she read a small piece of paper.

"What's that?" I said as I walked up to the lunch table to join her.

"A note," she said.

"From who?"

"Probably Johnny."

"Let me see it," I said, holding out my hand.

Gretchen gave it to me, then removed three others from her French book.

"You might as well see them all," she said quietly.

I spread the notes out on my lap out of sight of those around us. Each note was short, but hateful.

Maybe the Jap will stab you while you sleep.

Suppose he poisons the well.

Your mother and the baby will be alone in the house sometimes.

Jap lovers end up dead.

"Where did these come from?" I said.

"They're being slipped through the slits in my locker door."

"You have to tell somebody."

"No," she said firmly. "And don't you either."

I watched Gretchen wad the notes up tightly and drop them into the trash. I wished that Johnny's hate could be disposed of as easily as that.

Chapter 11

Despite my vow to pay closer attention to Pastor Patterson, I was having a terrible time concentrating on the Scriptures he was reading. A soft breeze wafted through an open window, bringing with it the smell of lilacs. The sun shining through the stained glass windows made shimmering designs on the wall behind the altar.

But the biggest distraction was the baby peeking over her daddy's shoulder in front of me. Her dark, gracefully slanted eyes shone as she looked all around the congregation. When her eyes rested on me, she grinned, showing two pearly bottom teeth.

I held my lips tightly together, trying not to smile back at her. Earlier I'd returned her grin. She'd bounced up and down on her daddy's lap and squealed. Several dozing members of the congregation had startled, and Pastor Patterson's eyes had flown up from the Bible. Right in front of me, her father's neck had reddened, and I'd heard Taylor laugh.

Even so, I was finding it extremely hard to ignore her. She was Miyo Kisaka, and she was attending the Methodist church in Hannah for the first time.

Before closing the service with the benediction, Pastor Patterson said to her parents, Thomas and Yuri Kisaka, "We're delighted to have you join our congregation, you and your lively daughter, who seems to like us already."

Turning to the congregation, he smiled broadly. "On Wednesday evening before choir practice and Bible study, there will be a potluck dinner to welcome the Kisakas. I trust all of you will attend."

My mouth watered. I couldn't help it. But I listened to every word of the benediction, trying to keep my face serious despite the joy in my heart.

As soon as the majority of the congregation left, several men, Papa too, began to load a borrowed truck with the furniture and other goods that had been collected at the church. Gretchen and I rode in the truck with Pastor Patterson while the Bochers, the Kisakas, and some others followed in cars. We unloaded onto the front porch of the little house.

After a picnic lunch under the trees in the orchard, Mr. Bocher, the expert organizer, delegated jobs. First, Mrs. Van Holt mopped the floor in each room. Then while J.L. and Miyo slept in a playpen on the porch, Mrs. Bocher and Yuri measured the three rooms in the little house to determine where the furniture should be placed. After Taylor and his mother polished each piece, a couple of men carried the furnishings inside. Gretchen and I wiped out the kitchen cupboards while some women washed the donated dishes and pans. Mama and some others dug up the area around the porch and planted marigold and zinnia seeds.

All afternoon Yuri and Thomas smiled at each other and at everyone else. Yuri touched each piece of furniture as if it were a family treasure rather than something carried out of a dusty attic somewhere in Cane County. She unpacked the bundle and two suitcases containing everything they owned. All of it fit into a chest of drawers and an old, battered armoire with plenty of space to spare.

By late afternoon, the house was organized and spotless. The adults left to look at the garden and the orchard while Gretchen and I sat on the floor in the living room, watching the babies crawl through each room.

"I can't believe it's finally happened," I said, feeling both tired and contented.

"You aren't half as happy as Thomas and Yuri. They're smiling all the time," Gretchen said.

* * *

Wednesday night as Mama and I packed the food basket with a scalloped potatoes and ham casserole, a cherry pie, and our tableware, the back porch door slammed. Papa rushed in. He jerked off his dusty jacket and sat down to unlace his work boots.

"I'm hurrying," he said before Mama could scold.

Mama paced the kitchen, glancing on each return trip at the clock. But Papa, true to his word, appeared in minutes, freshly scrubbed and wearing a clean shirt and trousers.

Picking up the basket, he offered Mama his arm. "Shall we go?"

He winked at me as we walked out to the car.

There were only eight cars at the church, which surprised me since I was sure we'd be the last ones to arrive. Inside, an unsmiling Pastor Patterson announced that we'd wait a bit for the others. Gretchen, Taylor, and I watched the minute hand on the clock inch to six-ten, then six-fifteen. At six-twenty, Pastor Patterson said the blessing, and we lined up to fill our plates. There was no deep-dish chicken pie from Mrs. Evans, nor any strawberries or rhubarb. There were only two desserts besides Mama's pie.

But there was the usual conversation about planting progress, gardening, and families. Thomas and Yuri seemed hesitant to join in, but they answered the questions people asked. Both were Los Angeles natives and had grown up in the same neighborhood. Neither had ever been out of California before the war. Yuri had been in nurse's training, and Thomas had finished a degree in history before their relocation. Thomas's two brothers were being held at Tule Lake in California. Thomas and Yuri had first been held at an assembly center near Los Angeles and then sent to Manzanar for about a year. Miyo had been born in an unsanitary, bare room at the infirmary with no doctor present.

I watched Thomas and Yuri as they answered the questions. Neither volunteered any more information than what each answer required. They were very solemn, not at all relaxed and smiling as they'd been on Sunday at the little house.

Miyo, on the other hand, was completely unreserved. She was right in the middle of the kids, her fine black hair standing up all over her head like a fuzzy dark halo. J.L., the twins, and Tessie Bensen were crawling around in a line with Miyo in the lead. Suddenly, she'd stop, change direction, and butt heads with J.L. He'd snort at her, then sit up and grin. When he reached for her hair, one of the twins grabbed his pudgy fingers. We wanted Miyo to like J.L., and his hair-pulling habit wouldn't help.

* * *

It was three weeks before I was positive that church attendance was down. No longer could the weather or spring colds be blamed. About a fourth of the congregation hadn't come to church since the Kisakas had attended.

When I mentioned it to Gretchen, she said I was borrowing trouble. Besides, she pointed out, those who were coming to church were eagerly helping the Kisakas. That was all that mattered.

She was right. The little house was well furnished. The pantry was stocked with enough canned foods and staples to last until the garden began to produce. Every week several people donated small amounts of precious meat, which was rationed.

Wanting to believe Gretchen, I vowed to worry less and study more since final exams were coming soon.

* * *

The last bus ride was noisier than usual. Exams were over, and there were many good-byes at each stop.

Because gasoline was strictly rationed, we expected to see even less of each other that summer than the previous one.

Gretchen and I and the little girls got off the bus in Hannah to meet Mrs. Bocher and Yuri, who were coming to town to get groceries and to run some errands. Betty Jean and Gloria walked with us toward the Piggly-Wiggly.

"Aren't you afraid to be seen with them?" Gloria said quietly to me as we approached the store.

"With who?"

"Those new people," she said.

Before I could respond, Gretchen waved and ran to meet her mother, Yuri, and the babies.

"People are talking," Betty Jean said.

"Let them talk," I said with more bravery than I felt. "Talk never hurt anyone."

Gloria shrugged. With eyes down, she and Betty Jean walked past Mrs. Bocher and Yuri and headed on home.

Joining the others, I took a sleeping J.L. from Mrs. Bocher and sat down on the bench in front of the grocery store. Gretchen, holding Miyo, marched up and down the sidewalk to amuse her and the twins. Several old men who'd been sitting on the bench in front of the barbershop got up and disappeared inside. Miyo was happily smiling at everyone who passed. A few people smiled back. Most, however, looked away. If Gretchen noticed, she didn't react. Pointing to one object after another, she said, "Tree, car, truck, lady," for Miyo's benefit.

A little girl and her mother stepped out of the store. "Was that the bad lady, Mommy?" the little girl said, pointing back inside.

The woman's face reddened when she saw Gretchen and Miyo. "Hush, now," she said, hurrying the little girl down the street.

"Who's a bad lady?" Carla said, peering into the store.

"There's no bad lady. It's just talk," Gretchen said, but her smile at Carla and Roberta was tight at the corners.

If Gretchen was worried, it didn't show once we got back to her house. Besides, within days, even I was almost too busy to worry.

Although our garden demanded many hours of my time, Mama allowed me to help the Bochers and the Kisakas whenever she could spare me. I'd convinced her, with Papa's help, that it was important to me to become involved with the mission project.

There was plenty to do. Thomas and Yuri were pruning the apple and peach trees in the neglected orchard and clearing the high weeds beneath them. Mr. Bocher was repairing a dilapidated chicken coop for the fifty chicks given to them by the congregation. All of us worked in the garden.

Gretchen and I also often took care of J.L. and Miyo. The two had become inseparable. They ate together, napped at the same time, and played on the floor when awake. Miyo knew how to pull herself up with the help of a chair or a table leg. She would stand, waiting for J.L. to join her. Then when he didn't, she'd plop back down, unwilling to be separated from him. I wondered if babies could be in love.

It was a busy, happy time as long as we stayed away from Hannah–and the stares.

* * *

Shortly after school was out, Taylor began walking down to our house several nights a week. I never knew when he might appear on our porch. As soon as dishes were done, I'd wash up, change clothes, and brush my hair, just in case. I tried to be nonchalant, but Mama caught on right away. One evening she came out onto the front porch where I was enjoying a rosy sunset and waiting.

"You're too young to date," she said.

"I know that," I said.

"Well, does Taylor?"

"Taylor is a friend. We've known each other since we were born."

"All the same, you may want to mention to him that you're only fifteen."

"For heaven's sake, he knows how old I am. Fifteen and a half."

I was glad for the approaching darkness since I knew my face was scarlet. Mama stood awhile, then went back inside. The bang of the screen door meant she'd dropped the subject, at least for that evening. I sat, letting my face cool.

Taylor did come. We sat on the steps, close, but not so close as to attract Mama's attention. We always had lots to talk about–his work, my work, the weather, stories about the babies and Gretchen, news from Eileen when letters arrived from Wyoming, and the latest war news, which was always grim.

When it was time for him to leave, I walked across the yard to the gate to say good-bye. That night Taylor took my hand and led me behind a spruce tree. Then, just as he had twice before, he took my face in his hands and kissed me.

"I love you, Joanna Elaine Grey," he said. "And someday you'll love me, too."

Then he disappeared into the darkness.

I didn't sleep much that night. Love in the movies seemed so easy to understand. A beautiful, elegantly dressed woman was pursued by a handsome man who brought her roses, took her to dinner, danced "sinfully close," Mama said, and kissed her passionately. People in love were never fifteen. The man never saw his beloved sitting mud-splattered in a cattail pond or crying at school or weeding rows of carrots.

The moon rose after midnight, flooding the pasture and garden with soft, white light. I wrapped my arms around my pillow and stared outside. A faint line of pink was streaking across the eastern sky before I finally closed my eyes.

* * *

When I arrived at the Bochers' house the next afternoon, Gretchen was already in the garden. I sat down at the opposite end of the bean row she was working on and began to pull weeds.

"Are you sick?" Gretchen said as we moved closer together.

I pulled another weed. "No, why?"

"You haven't said more than two words since you got here."

"I'm not sick."

"Well, what then?"

I pulled more weeds.

"I'm not trying to be nosy, but you don't look happy today," Gretchen said.

"But I am," I said, bursting into tears.

We quit weeding the beans. I dried my eyes on my shirttail. Then we sat cross-legged in the dirt while I told Gretchen that Taylor loved me.

When Yuri came out with water for us, she sat down beside me. "Why so serious?" she said, handing each of us a glass. "Telling secrets?"

I stared at the ground, but Gretchen said, "How did you and Thomas get together?"

"Oh, that subject," Yuri said, smiling. "Well, when I was ten, I decided that I'd marry him."

"And you told him?" I said, surprised.

"Not exactly," she said with a laugh. "I just made certain he knew I existed. Every time I saw him I spoke, and I made sure I saw him often. About ten years later, he finally spoke back. I'll let you figure out the rest."

Yuri stood up. "I need to check on the babies. By the way," she said with a smile, "Taylor is very good looking."

I stared at her as my face flamed. Then I smiled, too.

After Yuri left, Gretchen said she expected to fall in love but not until she was much older. She wasn't certain how to recognize love either, but she didn't believe it had much to do with flowers and fancy restaurants like in the movies.

"That's good since my life is pretty short of wine and roses these days," I said.

"You can be real sarcastic sometimes," she said, laughing at me.

She started weeding again. I wrote "Joanna Elaine Bensen" in the dirt with my finger. Then I pulled some weeds. I wrote "Mrs. Taylor Bensen" in the dirt, then pulled more weeds.

"I think it's love if good things are better if he's there, and bad things aren't so bad," Gretchen said. "You want the same things in life. You believe the same things are important. And when he kisses you–"

I looked up.

"He has kissed you," she said, grinning. "Your face is red. Taylor's already kissed you, hasn't he?"

I confessed. It felt good to sort out my jumbled feelings.

"Why can't you fall in love with a friend?" Gretchen said. "Maybe that's best. The question is, how do you feel when you see Taylor?"

"All warm and excited. I want to tell him everything that's happened since I last saw him. I want to know what he's been doing. When I see him walking up the lane, my heart beats faster."

"That's love," Gretchen said, sighing.

Suddenly, a shadow swept across the garden. We looked up. Dark clouds were rolling toward us. A gust of cooler air rustled the tree leaves in the orchard.

"I'd better leave," I said, rising quickly from the ground. "I can beat the storm home."

"Are you sure?" Gretchen said as I ran to my bicycle.

"Pretty sure," I shouted over the rising wind.

I waved with one hand as I started down the lane. I pedaled fast, keeping one eye on the rutted road and the other on the darkening sky. When I flew past the Conrad barn, I saw the rain falling in a heavy gray sheet in the distance. The race was going to be close. My heart pounding, I pedaled harder and harder, pushing against the wind. As I sped toward our pasture, I saw Papa driving in the cows.

"Get to the house," he said, yelling above the storm. "Your ma's worried. This is going to be a big one."

I wheeled my bike into the shed and latched the door firmly. A curtain of rain pounded the corn leaves as it raced across the field. Even though I was running as hard as I could, I got soaked before I reached the pump.

When the screen door slammed, Mama looked up from the kerosene lamps she was cleaning. The tight, worried look disappeared from her face. But as I stood in the kitchen doorway, making a puddle on the floor, she scolded me all the same.

"Good heavens, Joanna, you don't have the sense of a mule, or you'd come in out of the rain."

I bit my tongue.

"Now get out of those wet clothes before you catch your death. I need help with these lamps. You never know about the power."

The brief, furious thunder and lightning storm moved eastward, leaving behind it a slow, steady rain. After supper, I spent hours on the porch, listening to the gentle patter on the roof and leaves. I was hoping Taylor might come.

But Taylor didn't come that night, nor the next or the next since the rain continued for several days. When he finally did visit, Mama invited him inside for homemade ice cream and fresh raspberries. I didn't get a chance to go behind the spruce tree.

* * *

July got hot and steamy, each day like all the others. The corn shot up way over my head, and all the rain made weeds sprout overnight. We'd barely get done hoeing the last row in the garden before the weeds would be threatening to take over the first ones again.

Then it was August.

I knew something was wrong the minute Gretchen came to the screen door. Her face was very pale.

"Come on in," she said quietly, pointing at J.L. and Miyo, who were sleeping on soft mats on the living room floor.

As we tiptoed past them, I paused. Despite the gentle breeze blowing from the open west window, J.L. had tiny sweat beads across the bridge of his nose. Miyo's hair clung to her damp skin, fringing her face with wee dark spikes. A warm, peaceful feeling flooded my heart.

"Hi, precious babies," I whispered.

As I followed Gretchen upstairs to her room, I wondered at her silence.

"Do we need to work in the garden this afternoon?" I said once the door was closed.

She stared at me blankly.

"Gretchen, what's going on?" I said.

"I don't really know," she said, a catch in her voice. "That's what's wrong."

"Back up. Tell me from the beginning. What's happened?"

"All right, but you can't tell," she said.

"Not even Taylor?"

"Well, Taylor's okay, but nobody else."

Gretchen sprawled across her bed. I sat down in the rocker. Its creaking filled the silence.

"We got a hate letter yesterday postmarked from Hannah," Gretchen said finally.

"What did it say?"

"'We want you gone from here, you traitor whites and devil yellows. You got one week.' It was signed 'A Loyal American.'"

"Sounds like Johnny Crow," I said, my voice shaky.

"That's what Dad thought, too, until he showed it to Pastor Patterson. Turns out a couple of weeks ago his bishop received an anonymous letter that used the same words."

"A kid wouldn't write to a bishop," I said as my hands began to tremble.

I stopped rocking.

"Oh, God," I said more loudly than I'd intended. "You're going to have to move."

Gretchen's face crumbled. "I don't know."

I rushed to her, and we hugged and cried.

* * *

Pastor Patterson came that afternoon along with two carloads of parishioners. Different ones came with him the next day and the next.

Five days passed, then seven. The Bochers and the Kisakas didn't leave.

We halfheartedly weeded the garden. We forced ourselves to smile at church. We played with the babies and took Carla and Roberta to the cattail pond to wade. We tacked up more war headlines in the Conrad barn.

Rome Bombed by Allied Forces
90 Nazi U-Boats Sunk in 3 Months
120 Japanese Planes Destroyed
Canadians Occupy Kiska
Less Butter and Milk for Civilians
U.S. Casualties Now over 103,000
Estimated 100,00 out of 250,000 New U.S. Teachers
Hired Will Have Sub-standard Qualifications

Gretchen and Taylor received letters from Eileen, and we all wrote back to her. If the winter at Heart Mountain had been bad, the intensely hot, dry summer was even worse. Thousands of feet had turned the unpaved streets into powder. Winds whipped the dust through the same cracks that had let in the snow during the winter. Not sweeping, not dusting, not shaking could rid them of the grit. Her father had developed a hacking cough, sometimes choking and gasping for breath. Eileen was scared. We decided not to tell her about the threat in Hannah.

We counted day eight, ten, then fourteen.

Pastor Patterson dropped by every day or two, but no one else from the church came with him.

The tightness around my heart began to ease. The Bochers and the Kisakas smiled again. Thomas and Yuri started picking the early apples. We dug up the onions, put them into net bags, and hung them in the root cellar. I taught Gretchen how to make squash pie. We talked about school.

Four weeks passed without incident. I ripped the picture of the August gladiolus off our kitchen calendar, glad to be rid of that month. The September picture of grazing cattle against a cloudless blue sky was peaceful. That had to be a good omen.

Chapter 12

A cool dry breeze that was unusually pleasant for the second of September blew into the Conrad barn. Taylor had propped open the rickety door. I paced, holding a large manila envelope in my hand.

"Where can she be?" I said impatiently. "It's after three o'clock."

"She'll come if she can. Besides, we can't be positive she got her envelope today. We're only assuming they were mailed the same day."

"Of course, she got hers. We're all sophomores and Bensen and Grey came the same day. Why wouldn't Bocher?"

I walked to the doorway and looked down the empty lane.

"She promised to come as soon as she got her schedule so we can open our envelopes together like she and I did last year."

"Let's bike that way so you can move in one direction," Taylor said. "I'm getting dizzy watching you pace."

Taylor picked up his bicycle and rode away.

"Wait a minute," I shouted.

Taylor waved and pedaled on. I ran back into the barn, grabbed my manila envelope, and raced after him.

As we approached the Bochers' orchard, a striped ground squirrel scooted across the lane. I jerked my handlebars left to miss it and hit a half-buried rock. I yelled as my bike crashed and slid with my left leg caught beneath it.

Taylor knelt beside me, his face worried as he tried to brush the dirt off the long, bloody, skinned place below my knee.

"I was riding too fast," he said. "It's my fault."

I kept holding my leg while I squinched my eyes tight to keep back the tears. Blood trickled down to my socks.

"Can you stand up?" Taylor said.

He held out his hand. I got up slowly and hobbled to my bike. My leg was on fire.

"Oh, no," I said, pointing to the broken chain on my bicycle.

"We can walk. I'll go slow," Taylor said. "Gretchen's mom will bandage your leg."

We left my bike lying in the weeds and started walking. Taylor pushed his bike with one hand and held my hand with the other. I was trying hard not to limp. We were approaching the garden when I noticed the dust cloud.

"What's that?" I said, pointing toward Mill Pond Road.

"Don't know," Taylor said.

"It's too big for a tractor or a truck," I said.

We stopped to watch as it got nearer.

"I know what it is," Taylor said when the first vehicle appeared out of the cloud.

We stood motionless as the shapes of more and more cars and trucks became clear. My heart started to pound. I squeezed Taylor's hand as tears flooded my eyes.

"Oh my God, they've come after all," he said.

Taylor dropped his bike and pulled me between two rows of dried sweet corn stalks.

"Stay out of sight. I'm going to go get help."

"I'm going with you," I said, clutching his arm.

"You can't. Your bike's broken. I can ride faster without you."

"What will they do?" I said, my voice shaking as tears spilled down my cheeks.

We watched the first car turn slowly into the Bochers' lane.

"Probably nothing," Taylor said firmly, but his eyes were wide and his face pale. "I'm going for help just in case. Don't leave the garden."

Backing out of the corn, he ran, hunched down, to his bike, jumped on, and disappeared beyond the orchard.

My head throbbed, my leg throbbed. It was hard to breathe. Slowly, I crept to the end of the row nearest the house and lay flat on the ground.

The cars and trucks were pulling into a semicircle in the barn lot, all facing the house. More came–ten, twelve, fifteen. Groups of men were stepping out. I couldn't see their faces or much of their bodies because the vehicles were in the way. So many men, all bunched tightly together. The silence hung heavy.

A tall man in a battered straw hat stepped forward and yelled, "Hey, Bocher, get out here. We've got business with you."

There was no movement inside the house. I glanced toward the Kisakas' house. It appeared deserted, too.

My heart was pounding so loudly I was afraid it could be heard. I clutched my chest to muffle the sound.

"You want us to come get you and the Japs?" someone else in the crowd yelled.

Again, no movement. No sound.

"We warned you, traitor man. We want you gone, and today you're going to leave."

Please, God, make him stay inside, I begged silently.

But the screen door opened slowly, and Mr. Bocher stepped out. He moved to the edge of the porch, his sheet-white face expressionless. I thought of the way Gretchen had looked that day she was surrounded at the pump.

"But we're not hurting anyone," he said.

Loud yells came from the crowd.

Raising one hand, Mr. Bocher said, "Let me explain–"

"No words. Just leave," someone cried out.

The crowd became louder, more agitated. Mr. Bocher was still trying to talk, but I couldn't hear him.

A tomato flew through the air and smashed against the porch railing, splattering Mr. Bocher. Taking a handkerchief from his pocket, he wiped the pulp from his face and his shirt. He held up both hands.

"Please, let me explain," he shouted above the noise.

Another tomato splattered against the house. Then another and another. And with the tomatoes came more angry shouts from the crowd. "What are we waiting for? Get the Japs."

The rain of tomatoes continued.

"Hurry, Taylor. Please, God, help," I whispered over and over again.

Mr. Bocher was pleading, his hands outspread and his palms up. "We've no place to go. We have children," he yelled above the din.

"You can all go to hell," the tall man in the straw hat shouted back.

"Go to hell," was repeated throughout the crowd.

Mr. Bocher stepped back. The men, shoulder to shoulder, stepped forward.

I was breathing fast, but the air was too heavy. I looked down Mill Pond Road. No one was coming to help. The noise at the house got louder and louder.

The brick came hurtling from somewhere inside the mob. It arced up, bathed in brilliant sunlight, then plummeted down, crashing through the living room window.

There was silence. Then a scream. From inside the house came a long, heart-rending scream.

The screen door opened. Mrs. Bocher walked slowly to the edge of the porch holding J.L. to her breast. She stopped, her body immobile, while blood dripped from the hand that cradled his tiny smashed head.

I ran from the garden. That awful scream was inside my head. I didn't know if it was hers or mine. I stared at the red stain on her dress spreading wider and wider until

she and all the silent, motionless men looked bloody.
When I turned away, the sun in the sky was red, too.
And then I was falling.

* * *

I didn't open my eyes. I listened. Someone was
breathing nearby. I tried to remember where I was and
why I hurt so much.

When I opened my eyes, I saw the red and cried
out.

"You're home, Joanna. You're safe," Papa said
quietly.

"They hurt the baby," I said with a sob.

"I know, honey. Sleep now."

He wiped my face with a cool cloth, and I closed my
eyes. Papa was there each time I awoke all night.

The next afternoon I didn't object when Mama pulled
my nightgown over my head and helped me into a warm
bath. She shampooed my hair, scrubbed my back, and
carefully washed the raw sore on my leg. She laid out
clean clothes for me while I dried. Then she bandaged
my leg and helped me put on a summer dress. As we
sat on the porch swing, she brushed and towel-dried my
hair. Mama hadn't done that since I was little.

Then we drove to the cemetery.

The hole in the ground was tiny. So was the coffin that went into it. Bits of late afternoon sunlight filtering through the tree leaves danced all around us. But the sunlight couldn't reach into the bottom of that hole. It was very dark down there.

I saw Gretchen, her eyes wide and dry. She didn't seem to see me or Taylor or anyone there. All the Bochers stood that way, their flaming hair unnaturally bright for the deathly pallor of their faces.

I was having trouble hearing. I stared at Pastor Patterson. His hands holding the Bible were shaking, and there were dark shadows all around his eyes. His mouth moved, but I couldn't understand the words.

Everything was turning red. I swayed. Papa's arm tightened around me. The red faded, but I couldn't stop the tears. Through the blur, I saw Mr. Bocher step to the edge of the hole and push a plain wooden cross into the soft earth. Yuri laid an armful of white daisies beside it. Miyo raised her head sleepily from her father's shoulder and whimpered.

Slowly, we walked back to our car.

* * *

"I thought you might come here," Taylor said. He was sitting on a large flat rock in front of the Conrad barn.

"Were they at church?" I asked.

He shook his head.

I felt my eyes filling with tears. He reached for my hand and pulled me down to sit beside him.

"They're gone, Joanna. Dad says the place is deserted. Pastor Patterson is gone, too. There was a lay minister this morning."

I couldn't stop the sobs. I buried my face on Taylor's shoulder and cried.

"There's something inside for you," he said after my tears stopped.

We walked into the barn. In the dim light, I saw a package wrapped in brown paper lying on a dusty stool. I knew what it was before I opened it.

"It's the book I gave J.L."

With tears running down my face again, I took off the paper and held the book to my chest.

"Did she leave a note?" Taylor said.

I sat down, opened the book, and carefully turned each page. Between H and I was a folded sheet of stationery.

"I can't," I said, handing it to Taylor.

He unfolded the letter and read it aloud.

Dear Joanna,

Why did it end like this? What monstrous evil could want that precious baby to die? Will I ever understand?

We're leaving. Dad says that it's best that I don't know where or even how we'll go. We won't be back. He says it won't be safe for me to write you or you to write me. Pastor Patterson has already taken Thomas, Yuri, and Miyo away.

I'll never forget you, Joanna. I want you to have your ABC book because someday you'll have your own baby who will love its colorful pictures. Teach your baby that H should stand for horse, not hate.

It's time to go. Dad's been packing. I must help him. Mother only sits and stares.

> *Your friend forever,*
> *Gretchen*

P.S. When you go to the cemetery, will you tell J.L. that I love him?

We were outside in the sunshine all the rest of that afternoon–talking some, sitting in silence a lot. Taylor told me that when he went for help, he'd found his dad in the pasture repairing a fence. They'd gotten the car and driven to the closest phone to call the sheriff and Pastor Patterson.

When Taylor and his dad got to the Bochers' house, all the men were gone. The only signs of what had happened were the trampled grass in the barn lot, the smashed tomatoes on the house, and Mrs. Bocher.

"She was sitting on the porch steps with blood all over her, so still she didn't look alive," Taylor said so softly that I turned toward him to listen. There were tears streaming down his cheeks. "I didn't realize she was holding J.L. until we got closer. Oh, God, Joanna, all that blood was his!"

Taylor's head dropped to his arms, which were folded across his knees. He sobbed. I put my arm across his shoulders until he brushed away the tears.

"Dad told me not to go any closer. He walked on and I ran to find you. I saw Gretchen first, sitting in the garden, not moving. Then you, sprawled in the dirt beside her. She was holding your hand. I was so relieved to see you were breathing."

Taylor reached for my hand. I thought of what Gretchen had said about love. Bad things wouldn't be so bad if he was there.

"Dad found Thomas, Yuri, and the little girls hiding in the storm cellar near the barn, safe but in shock. Inside the house, Miyo was still asleep near where J.L. had been, and Mr. Bocher was dashing frantically from room to room, gathering things to put into boxes and suitcases, trying to pack. Dad said he'd pick up a single shoe and a couple of books and put them into a box, then pull out a dinner plate from the same box and put it into a suitcase."

There wasn't much more to tell. Pastor Patterson and some parishioners arrived at the same time the sheriff did. Mr. Bensen carried me to their car and left. When they got to my house, Papa met him and carried me inside.

* * *

Several days later Taylor walked my broken bicycle to the house with my manila envelope in the basket. We looked at our sophomore schedules. Mine was damp and blurry since it'd lain in the weeds for several days before Taylor thought to get it. I hadn't remembered it at all.

Then school started. Not a soul mentioned Gretchen or J.L. or the Kisakas—as if all of them had never existed.

That included Old Henry. But when I boarded the bus the first morning, he looked right at me and said,

"Morning, Missy." He continued to speak to me every day.

Mama didn't talk about them either, but I discovered she'd put flowers on J.L.'s grave when I saw chrysanthemums there in a vase that used to be in the cupboard on our back porch. Whenever Taylor and I biked to the cemetery, I touched the little cross and blew J.L. kisses from Gretchen and me.

We didn't go back to the Conrad barn. It was too sad. The happy memories there had been buried by the sad ones, and I didn't want to see the newspaper stories about the war anymore.

In late September, Papa went with me to the county seat to answer questions before a coroner's jury even though I hadn't seen the men's faces nor recognized any voices. The jury ruled J.L.'s death a negligent homicide by person or persons unknown. The case remained unsolved.

My heart beat a bit faster in anticipation every time I opened our mailbox, but a letter never came.

On November fourteenth, Taylor got a short note from Eileen. In one sentence, she thanked us for our letters, and in another, she asked us not to write her again. She didn't mention Gretchen at all.

That evening I sat on the floor at my bedroom window, staring across the bare fields bathed in rosy light from the setting sun. As the peach and lavender near the horizon deepened into orange and purple and the remaining rays made the undersides of the high clouds glow, I cried.

J.L. would have been a year old that day.

Epilogue

I'd just dashed to the top of the stairs when the phone rang. I paused to see if it was our ring–one short, one long–before running back down.

"I'll get it," I said to Grandma Grey even though she'd made no move to answer the phone herself.

"Have you gotten your mail?" Taylor said.

"Not yet."

"Go get your bike. I'll meet you at the mailbox."

"I don't have time for a bike ride," I said. "Grandma's about ready for me to try on my dress again. It's gorgeous. You're going to love it."

"Only if it's blue."

I couldn't see Taylor's face, but I could picture his teasing smile. I laughed.

"I really need to see you," he said, suddenly sounding serious. "It's important."

"Okay, but only for a little while. I'll be right there."

I went up to my room to brush my hair and to put a daub of powder on my nose. Then I walked into the living room where Grandma was sitting in an armchair near the window. With tiny stitches, she was hemming the silky pale blue skirt of my graduation dress.

Leaning down, I whispered conspiratorially in her ear. "Taylor wants to see me. I'll try to be back before Mama misses me."

Grandma looked up and winked. I giggled.

"Love you," I said, kissing her on the cheek.

When I walked outside, I spotted Mama kneeling on the far side of the garden, planting green beans in a long straight row. I thought about yelling at her to tell her where I was going but thought better of it. I backed my bike out of the shed and headed down the lane without glancing back.

Taylor was waiting for me.

"Here's your mail," he said, dropping it into my basket.

He took off down the road, and I followed. When he didn't turn at the next corner, I knew we were going to the cemetery. I still touched the little cross and blew a kiss to J.L. each time we went there, but it hurt less. All my angry tears hadn't brought him back that first winter. When spring came with its rainbow of colors, the memory of his precious face began to push out the red and the pain and to fill me instead with the warmth I'd felt when I rocked him. Whenever I visited the cemetery, I hoped that somewhere Gretchen was also remembering her baby brother alive and smiling.

We stopped under the ancient elm tree that shaded the entrance to the cemetery, propped up our bikes, and walked in. There were bouquets of peonies by J.L. and Cy's graves. During the years since J.L. died, Mama had never mentioned the Bochers, the Kisakas, or the tiny grave, but the flowers were there from early spring until the first frost in the fall.

Taylor and I walked hand-in-hand back to our bikes.

"Is something wrong?" I said.

"Here," he said, pulling an ivory-colored envelope from the stack of mail in my basket.

I frowned at him, puzzled. "I don't understand."

"You will," he said, trying to hide a smile. "Open it."

I looked at the return address–C.T.B. from Chicago. I glanced at Taylor, who was smiling. As I slowly opened the envelope, my hands began to shake. I dared not hope.

"Read it," Taylor said, his eyes bright.

"It's from Gretchen–Carrot Top Bocher," I said, hugging him tight. "How did you know?"

"She wrote me, too," he said, withdrawing an identical envelope from his pocket.

We sat down beneath the old tree, shoulders touching. I began to read my letter, my heart pounding in my ears.

> *You can't know how long I've wanted to write you. It wasn't safe for us, or you. And my mother, well, she couldn't bear the thought of Hannah for a long time. But she's better now that the war's over.*
>
> *I picture you and Taylor together. I have written each of you, hoping that you'll meet to read these letters. If I'm wrong about you still loving each other–surely I'm not wrong–will you at least share my letter with him? Are you blushing? I hope so!*

I looked at the ring that Taylor had given me–a pale blue stone set in a graceful golden swirl. I had belonged to his grandmother.

"You're blushing," Taylor said. "Aren't you going to share your letter with me? You're supposed to."

"How do you know?"

"Because you love me, and Gretchen wants me to share mine with you," he said, giving me a quick kiss.

Taylor held my hand while I read the rest of the letter aloud.

> *We lived in Wisconsin a year, then moved back to Chicago—but not at the address on the front of the envelope. That's for Groman's Fish Market. Mother's still afraid that someone in Hannah might see our address, and I go along with her most of the time. Our real address is on the last page. We're sharing a house with my grandma. Please write me.*
>
> *Dad got a job after the war as an assistant editor for a small magazine. Mother does volunteer work with disabled children. I'm graduating soon and going into nurse's training in the fall. Carla and Roberta will be in fifth grade next year, so tall you'd hardly recognize them.*
>
> *We don't talk about Hannah. It's like that year and a half doesn't exist. I know*

Carla and Roberta suffered when J.L. died. Not only was he gone, but Mother withdrew into silence, and Dad was hardly aware of us. During the first months, both the girls had nightmares. I'd get up to pat them on the back, but I didn't know how to make them feel better, or me either.

I try to picture J.L. as going on four, but I can't. He's forever a baby who wrinkled up his nose and grinned at me.

The Kisakas are also in Chicago. We visit every once in awhile, but I think they blame themselves for what happened to J.L. Sometimes I think my dad blames himself since the whole project was his idea. I wonder if it would've made any difference if I'd told about Johnny Crow like you wanted me to.

Enough melancholy.

Miyo is adorable, not the tiniest bit shy like Thomas and Yuri. Because she has no memory of what happened, she's the only one who's free from the shadow that hangs over us whenever we're together. The first time we visited them after we moved back to Chicago, she carted a big teddy bear into the living room, plopped him down on Mother's lap, demanding that she hold him, and left. Thomas and Yuri were mortified. I guess they feared it would hurt Mother to see Miyo growing up. A few minutes later, Miyo returned with a book. She crawled up on Mother's lap. Yuri jumped up to get her, but Mother said she wanted to read to Miyo and her bear. They've been special friends since.

Well, that fills in the past few years. I've written you a thousand times in my head. Now that the words are down on paper they seem so ordinary and bare of all the feelings I have. I think about you and Taylor all the time. I want to know absolutely everything that's happened!

Laying the letter in my lap, I leaned my head back against the tree and closed my eyes. A slight breeze rustled the leaves high up.

"I thought you'd be happy," Taylor said.

"I am."

"You don't look it," he said, sounding worried.

"Trust me, I am."

I opened my eyes and looked at his solemn face. I still marveled that anyone could love me so much.

"I'd given up ever knowing what happened to Gretchen," I said. "After D-Day, I began writing a letter to her every week. I hid them all in a box in my closet. I was so positive Gretchen would write since the war was ending, and I wanted to tell her about everything, like Jeremiah surviving and Johnny and his folks moving across the state to be near the veterans' hospital, and Grandma coming to live with us, and my beautiful blue ring. I wanted to have all the news ready as soon as I had her address."

"So you're going to send Gretchen the letters."

"I can't." I paused, fighting back the tears. "When I didn't hear from her by Christmas, I burned them."

Taylor put his arm around me, and I snuggled against his shoulder, clutching the letter to my chest.

"I can't believe she's finally written," I said.

After awhile, I jumped up, grabbed Taylor's hands, and pulled him to his feet. We twirled around, laughing.

Suddenly, I stopped. "She didn't mention Eileen."

"Yes, she did," Taylor said, pulling his letter out of his pocket.

"Don't read it. Tell me quick," I said. "We can read it all later."

"It's not good," he said, his smile gone. "Eileen, David, and their mother were released as soon as the war ended."

"Not her father?"

Taylor shook his head. "He died at Heart Mountain in 1944. Pneumonia."

"Still a prisoner," I said softly.

"Gretchen said Eileen is bitter. After the war ended, all the people in the camps were told to leave, to go wherever they chose. But there was nothing for the Matsuyamas in California except bad memories, so they headed east and ended up in Cincinnati, where David found a job in a lab. Mrs. Matsuyama cooks in a little café. Eileen's working in a library. She wants to go to college, but there's no money. They left Heart Mountain with nothing but train fare and the clothes they wore."

"They're having to start all over," I said.

Taylor didn't answer.

We reached for our bikes and began walking them toward home.

"Taylor, do you remember the story of Pandora?"

"The myth?" he said, looking puzzled.

"Yes. Pandora's curiosity made her open the box and let out all the evils in the world except one–foreboding."

"Why are you thinking about her now?"

"After J.L. died, I thought about how unbearable it would've been if we'd known ahead of time what was going to happen to him. It would destroy people to know the future, wouldn't it?"

"I guess so," he said.

"This way people have hope," I said. "I can hope and pray there's never another war. I can hope Eileen goes to college. I can hope we get to see Gretchen some day. I can hope you'll always be with me."

"Of course, I'll be with you."

"We can't know that for sure."

Taylor stopped walking and looked at me. Then a mischievous grin broke out on his face. He jumped on his bicycle.

"If you're going to be with me, you'll have to catch me first," he said over his shoulder.

"Hey, I haven't read your letter yet," I said, racing after him.

A Note from the Author

One fall afternoon in 1982, I drove from my middle-school teaching job to a seed corn plot demonstration sponsored by the agricultural company where my husband was a sales manager. While there, I started talking to an elderly man I hadn't met before. During the conversation, he mentioned where he'd grown up. It sounded like he'd lived close to the remodeled one-room schoolhouse where I was raised and still live, so I asked him if he knew my dad. The man's response chilled me. "I haven't seen your father since the night of the lynch mob."

I knew what he was referring to—a part of my family history that had occurred when I was an infant. In the summer of 1943, my father had gone to Chicago to see about resettling a Japanese-American family on our down-state Illinois farm. A Quaker group had been working to obtain the release of some families from the internment camps in the West. With the backing of the local Methodist minister, Dad brought a family to the community—a father, a mother, and a nine-year-old boy.

When reactions in the community became negative, Dad asked people to meet at the country schoolhouse, which became our home later, so that he could explain how he and Mom intended to share the farm income with the family. A mob assembled, but it took no action since some of Dad's friends who'd heard some talk in town beforehand called the sheriff. Even though tragedy was averted, the anger was so strong that Dad took the family back to Chicago.

I had learned bits and pieces of the story while growing up. I remember a visit with the family in Chicago when I was in grade school and a time when the father came to our house and wrote a message in Japanese in my autograph book. But I don't remember ever hearing the words "lynch mob."

The next time I visited my parents in California, where they'd moved with my two sisters in the mid-1960s, I asked my dad to tell me the whole story. Later, I received a copy of a long, nine-page, typed letter he'd written to a family friend immediately after the events in 1943. I also have the Methodist minister's autobiography which describes his memory of the events.

I did research about the 1940s and the war, specifically about the internment camps for the ethnic Japanese. The history in the novel is real, but all the characters, the town of Hannah, and the events that unfolded there are purely fiction. The message about the evil of prejudice, however, is forever relevant—maybe even more so since the attack of 9/11 when for a brief time some people suggested that the government should consider internment camps for Muslims living in this country. Once again, I was chilled by the words of others—and more determined than ever to tell this story so that more people will know what was done during World War II and will feel as I do that mistakes, such as those described in *When the War Came to Hannah,* should never be made again.

About the Author

Jane S. Creason lives with her husband in a remodeled one-room schoolhouse, where she has lived since she was four years old. They have two adult children, both married, and four grandchildren. After earning bachelor's and master's degrees from the University of Illinois, she taught at the grade school, middle school, and high school levels before retiring in 1994. Since then, she has been a part-time English instructor and director of the Writers' Room at Danville Area Community College. Having lived in the same house with the same husband and taught English in the same county for much of her life, Jane describes herself as a contented Midwesterner who has put down serious roots.